I0658525

Bella Butterfly

Marie van-Doorn

Copyright © 2025 by Marie van-Doorn

All rights reserved.

No part of this publication may be reproduced, distributed, or transmitted in any form or by any means, including photocopying, recording, or other electronic or mechanical methods, without the prior written permission of the publisher, except as permitted by U.S. copyright law. For permission requests, contact the publisher via email lynnejlloyd@outlook.com.

Edited by Lynne Lloyd at LLOYD MOSS PUBLISHING www.lloydmoss publishing.com

ISBN 978-1-763742727

Dedication

To both my mothers and my fathers. Without their shared experiences, this story would never have been told.

'Life must be lived forwards but can only be understood backwards.'

–Søren Kierkegaard ~ philosopher

Contents

Chapter One

Leaning over the high railing, Nico could not take his eyes off the two tug boats pulling their ship away from the wharf. Like the ship, he was breaking ties from the land of his birth and from his traditional Italian family, most likely forever. He was rejecting the life his father had mapped out for him.

Nico would forge his own path in the world. Beside him on the crowded aft deck was the woman he chose out of love, not duty. His Ava stood so close it was as if they were one. Her arm looped over his arm, her hand firmly clasped his hand.

Young and in love, Nico and Ava had eloped from their homes in northern Italy. They were on the greatest adventure of their lives, moving to a new country on the other side of the world. It was exciting and a little terrifying. Apart from its name, they knew nothing about Australia. What would it be like? It would be a whole new existence. A journey to an unknown future.

It had been a long six weeks of staring at the relentless ocean waves, punctuated with an occasional stopover at a foreign port. They had wandered through the same shops and eaten the same unfamiliar food in the ship's dining room. Their enthusiasm and high hopes slipped slowly away. With too much time to think, doubt crept into their minds: "Had they been too rash?" They looked back in the direction of their beloved Europe which was further away with every passing day.

Bleak clouds appeared on the horizon and icy wind blew shards of misty brine through every crevice in the old ship. Nico and Ava felt the piercing frigid fingers penetrating their bones as the ship rounded the Cape of Good Hope. They caught fleeting glimpses of Africa's distant coastline.

Even in the cabins it was bitterly cold and the musty smell of the sea lingered everywhere, burning nostrils and churning stomachs.

Unperturbed, the huge migrant carrier creaked and groaned as it was borne from one rolling wave to another. Apathy and motion sickness were the norm and human tolerance was pushed to its limit. For many, it was a brave journey to a new world. For some, it piqued their pioneering instincts and was tinged with adventure. For others like Nico and Ava, it was a way of putting the past behind them. A way to distance themselves from a life they feared, a life they wanted to run from.

They finally left Africa behind them as the ship set course for Australia. The last part of the journey was uneventful, four weeks of smooth sailing under a blazing sun as the ship slid gracefully over the glassy waters.

The trip was almost over. Tensions were running high. Everything about their surroundings irritated them. The ship was now claustrophobic.

The same blank faces stared out over the expansive waters searching the distant horizon for any signs of land. Day after day, night after night. Sunrise, sunset and sunrise again. Nothing changed.

The young honeymooning couple had rarely ventured from their first class but sparse cabin. But on the second leg of their voyage, from time to time, Nico and Ava became impatient with each other. One day, they were quarrelling and their raised voices drifted into the narrow corridor outside the couple's cabin.

"Ava," Nico growled huskily, with malice fuelled by his frustration, "we need to find somewhere to live first. How can you expect me to support a pregnant wife with no job, no money and no home? A baby can wait." Nico's long fingers raked through his coarse black mane. He grabbed a fistful of hair, pulling it away from his scalp, "We have hardly any money left, all my savings went on this trip. Do you forget .... my family disowned me? I no longer have an inheritance. I must find a way to support us," he shouted.

His voice dropped and became gentle again, "We can do this, but we need to do it together."

Ava blinked slowly. He could see her despair as a single tear fell from her eye. His voice rose again, "We need a home and I need a job. Then we can think about a family."

They had argued many times previously. He hated seeing his beautiful fragile wife so forlorn. It triggered feelings of anger and inadequacy in him. He was used to having everything fixed around him with money and comforts which was how it was in his wealthy family. His family and position meant he never had to worry or want for anything.

It all changed when he chose to go against his family's custom and follow his heart instead of marrying a woman who had been chosen for him. The woman chosen was from another prestigious wine family who would strengthen the generations-old family business and ensure its future. But Nico loved Ava and Ava idolised him.

Nico was tired of arguing about the same thing and his voice became fierce, "For God's sake, Ava, you're only twenty-two. What's the hurry?"

His open hand struck the wall above the wash basin over which his wife was leaning. She winced, and spat angrily into the sink.

Slamming the toothbrush back into the case, Ava turned to face him, expecting to see his face reddened and his eyes blazing. The fire in her pale blue eyes flickered slightly as she recognized the core of what had initially attracted her to him. It was a mixture of masculine brutality and tenderness. It was a quality rarely found in Italian men, but it was beautifully blended into the essence of Nico Palladino.

"I feel I need a baby," she whispered hoarsely, "I am sure we would manage, and you would make a wonderful father and—"

"We need a house," he hissed, cutting her off. "We don't even know what town we'll be living in. How can a baby be so important when we don't even have a home?"

His comment provoked her once again and she brought up his family, knowing, but not caring, that it was a futile argument and would only serve to pour more fuel on his anger. "Your uncle promised to get us off to a good start .... he said he would get the money you were entitled to and..."

"No!" Nico growled vehemently, his hot breath in her face, the venom in his voice made her feel he was dismissing her needs as unimportant.

His passion caused him to become more animated, and he raised his voice again, "You are my family; you are my wife! I will not accept any money not given willingly by my father." Slamming his open hand against the wall, he added in a deep growl, "My family will never interfere in my life again."

"But...." she muttered almost under her breath, her body was slumped over on the bed, her voice quivering, "my mother asked before we left that we make her a Nonna quickly."

She was close to tears but he ignored her distress. He glared at her with open hostility, too embittered to care that tears were welling in her eyes and her lip was trembling.

"Your mother can wait, like you can wait. A baby is not so damned important that we need to start right away," he emphasised with a guttural growl. He looked at her, stretched out on the bed and weeping, and began to soften.

It was his family he despised, not Ava, and again his hatred had caused him to hurt the one person he loved more than anyone or anything. He cursed silently, and with his voice returning to its usual mellow timbre, he attempted to salvage what was left of his self-respect. "Ava, we don't know what town we'll be living in. I don't know much about Australia, but I do know that our home will not be anything like the vineyard, or your village for that matter. A baby will just complicate everything."

Nico sat gently beside her and reached out to touch her. She flinched, his touch felt like fire upon the icy coldness of her skin. Hurt by the rejection, he became angry once again. "What about work? I don't know what I'll be doing, I don't even know if I'll get a job straight away. Do you think that is any way to bring up a child, Ava?"

He lent over her body which was shaking with her sobbing and spoke gently, "Look at yourself, Ava, you're still a child yourself. You need to grow up a bit more. We need to grow up a bit more, get used to being married. Wake up, we need to sort out our life first before we even think about being responsible for another."

She knew he was right, but she was hurt which was evident by the racking sobs which were now out of control. "Sure," she said convulsively, "a baby isn't the most logical thing, but it feels so right, a child, our child, an heir to the Palladino Vineyards.... a grandchild .... a family."

He closed his eyes and his mind flicked back to another argument. He recalled his father's words, "You will never leave the vineyard, you are a Palladino. You will stay and produce Palladino sons. Our name will always be spoken of with awe and respect in Italy. Our heirs will stay in Italy!" He remembered the bitter fights. He hated the vineyards; he hated the lifestyle and most of all he resented the discipline of being a part of the oppressive Palladino family.

His father stated finally that, if he left for Australia, he could consider himself disinherited. There would be enough to ensure that any children would be comfortable but, as far as Nico and Ava were concerned, it would be as if they never existed. His mind snapped back to the present. "I will tell you this just once more," Nico repeated the solemn promise made to his father, "I will never return to the vineyards, NEVER .... and neither will my sons!"

Ava shrank away from him, stepping backwards. His face changed. She had never done that before. He was taken aback when he realized his young bride mistrusted his feelings for her. She wondered why his family always invoked such a passionate response, but he interpreted her reaction as fear.

Nico was instantly sorry he allowed his anger to compromise the security of their marriage. He vowed to put the family behind him, to concentrate on the present and the future and forget the past which only caused bitterness and anger.

His eyes begged for her forgiveness as his arms hung limply by his sides. He made no attempt to touch her as she skirted the wall and did not flinch when she slammed the door behind her. He simply touched his fingertip to his face and wiped away the silent tear sliding down his cheek.

"Palladino men don't cry," he heard his father's voice echoing in his head from when he was ten years old.

"She's gone!" his father yelled. "She won't come back. You are the eldest. One day the vineyards will be yours. You need to be strong for your sister and work with me in the vineyard. I will teach you like my father taught me and we will pass our legacy onto the next generation. We will continue to show what it means to be a Palladino in Italy."

That was twenty-one years ago, and the woman who died was his mother and his father yelled and told him not to cry. How he despised his father who was responsible for the pain suffered by all the women in his life.

Chapter Two

In another cabin, little Chiara tried one way after another to arrange her mass of black curls. Every time the boat lunged sideways, they kept falling over her face.

She squinted at her reflection in the tiny mirror and pulled the annoying mass of curls up again. The boat rolled on a large wave and yet again they fell down into her eyes. Thrown off balance, she finished up on the corner of the bed with her hair veiled across her face like a dirty black mop.

Throwing her head back, she muttered obscenities under her breath. From the corner of her eye, she spotted her mother's knitting bag sitting untouched by the bed since leaving Italy.

"Hmm," she mumbled under her breath as she slid to the floor, glancing at the mute figures of her parents by the porthole window. Gina and Enzo were staring blankly across the water which is what they did all day, every day. They cared little about what their daughter was doing inside the cabin and even less about what she was doing elsewhere. All they cared about was getting off this damned awful boat that had become their prison and starting afresh in Australia.

Chiara lifted herself from the floor and contemplated her features in the mirror. Hidden beneath the mop of black curls was a face of striking invulnerability. She saw a deep olive complexion darkened by years of roaming the streets and molten chocolate eyes which reflected a profound wisdom and an intense perception of the people and the world around her.

Interestingly, what was not evident was the childishness and vivacity of youth which one would expect from a child of thirteen. She exuded an ageless, timeless persona. A metaphysical all-knowing presence provided her with insightfulness. She could understand most people better than they could understand themselves and the comment often heard was that Chiara had been on this earth forever. Her mother often said, "She is a witch from the dark ages who the gypsies planted into our family. Our child could never be like this."

Only a few short years ago Chiara was an introverted little girl living in her own world and she was now an adolescent woman-child who was wise beyond her years.

The rolling water showed no signs of land. Gina was fighting a sickening thought that they were traveling in circles upon the ocean. They rounded the base of Africa three weeks ago and she could not understand why they had not yet reached Australia. "Surely there should be some sign of land by now," she mused. "We should have stayed in Rome!" she said to no one.

The street stall at least provided them with an income. It was her life and, as simple as it was, she enjoyed it. "Damn you, Enzo," she silently cursed for the tenth time that morning. "Why did he get involved with those men in the first place? If it were not for them, her life would be the same. Instead, here she was, forced to run away like a scared rabbit to another country.

"Damn you, Enzo," she cursed again, as she glared at him on the opposite side of the window. "Because of you we've got nothing, just this stupid cabin, on this stupid boat and going to a country I never wanted to go to in the first place."

Enzo continued to stare at the sea. He had lost his last shred of dignity when those men burnt his home to the ground and threatened his wife and child. His morale lay somewhere in the cinders of his house which had once been his sanctuary.

Gina continued to glare at her husband. The man she married had been strong, capable, and loved life. She detested this defeated wreck standing beside her. Each time she looked at what he had become: an unshaven, unkempt pile of impotence, her hatred and resentment grew stronger.

"That's better," Chiara announced, breaking rudely into her parents' reverie.

Gina whirled around to find her daughter standing with her knitting scissors in one hand and a mass of black curls clutched firmly in the other.

She gazed in stunned silence for a second at the patch where the hair used to be and then at the nonchalant face of her child.

Finally, the frustration she had been harbouring for weeks exploded and she screeched incoherently at her child. "You little witch!" she screamed, as she lunged for the scissors. Enzo caught her just in time as their daughter darted for the door, grabbing her father's overcoat. She slipped out, leaving her mother's furious ravings rattling down the narrow corridor.

Not once did she hear her father's voice over the commotion. This was unusual; he was usually the more spirited of the two. Lately, she mused, he appeared to be nothing more than a shell, having become detached from life since they left Italy. More than once, she wondered why they were making this journey.

She reflected on the day that everything changed. She came home from school and the house was gone; the fire had destroyed everything. The street stall was nowhere to be seen and her parents had disappeared. Bewildered and shocked, she ran to the hotel from which she had often dragged her happy and slightly inebriated father home.

Quickly, she was ushered to a basement cellar and into a makeshift home secreted behind the racks of wine deep in the bowels of the hotel. Gina and Enzo were sitting on a mattress behind a large rack of wines, two suitcases beside them and a gun on the floor.

That night she slept between her parents on the mattress and for three weeks they never left the cellar. Food was brought to them, extra clothing in a smaller suitcase for Chiara, trips to the bathroom after closing. Money, documents, and hushed conversations took place with late night visitors. There was never any explanation, no discussion with her about why they were hiding, or why the house had been burned, not even the opportunity for her to stay with relatives.

Three weeks of silence in that damp, cold cellar punctuated by secret strangers and hushed whispers while her mother sat in stony silence with her knitting needles, bag of wool and half-finished scarf. The gun was always lying close by.

When they finally left, it was to board the ship for Australia. Chiara didn't even have the chance to say good-bye. She missed her school friends; she missed the gypsies who were her kindred spirits; she missed the old pigeon woman who educated Chiara to the ways of the world; and, most of all, she missed her independence.

As she wandered along the ship's corridor, dragging her fingers across the polished hardwood hallway, she thought about her father and how small he had become.

The thought hit her even more as she slipped on his overcoat. He was a big man and she was still quite small. The coat enveloped her completely, the surplus dragging along the floorboards. She kept walking until she reached the upper deck.

She saw what she was looking for - the circle of deadpan faces and hunched backs around a table on the deck. These card players did not intrigue her like the gypsies did but they offered the unquestioning acceptance she was accustomed to.

The fine mist of salt soaked into the cards, making them soggy and difficult to shuffle, but still she managed, dealing five to each person and then five to herself. She was an experienced poker player and this time the pot in the middle consisted of five cigarettes. She tossed in a coin she retrieved from her father's pocket and threw in three of her cards. After dealing everyone a second hand, she looked at her own. Three sixes, an ace and a two. "What the hell," she thought and tossed in the one and only cigarette from a box in another pocket.

None of the faces had any hint of expression, but then they never did. She accepted them for what they were and they accepted her the same way. They did not acknowledge the little girl behind the tough exterior; all they cared to see was the ageless mind and a free roaming spirit beneath a mysterious facade which appeared to want nothing more than to get on with life in her own carefully construed way.

After realizing she had won, she took the contents of the centre, which was now seven cigarettes and two more coins and carefully tucked six of them into the packet, leaving one coin in the centre and another in front of her. The remaining cigarette she placed in her mouth, lit it and carefully looked at the cards in front of her. Without emotion, she threw them all aside.

Mario, who was now dealing, had a timeworn expression and a furrowed frown etched deeply into his features. His brother Guido had a face that seemed to have been carved from stone. She was sure that neither of them ever smiled because of the lack of wrinkles around their mouths. From the glazed expression in their eyes, she was sure that neither of them knew what it was to have a soul.

There was a woman in her forties whom she had never met before, a younger man with leathery skin and a bald head and a young woman who was hanging off him. She was not playing and Chiara suspected that this woman was soliciting business as she had seen her several times during the journey and each time with a different man.

She looked across at the rolling sea, and then at the five new cards which appeared in front of her. "I'm out," she announced as she surveyed the faces around her. She noted that the one thing they had in common was a haunting lack of expression. For a fleeting instant, she was suspended in time. She saw herself reflected in the eyes of each face, but not as herself, as an old lady. Old and emotionless and ravaged by time. She blinked, until she could again see the vague shadows of apathy on each face.

She stepped up silently from the game, threw the cigarette stub over the rail and ambled along the deck. The wind and the salty mist was particularly biting this morning. She pulled the coat tighter around her body. She chided herself for not putting shoes on before she left, but then she remembered, she left in a huge hurry. It was too soon to return yet; her mother would still be fuming.

Every now and then the overpowering stench of salt and fish invaded her nostrils and nauseous bile rose into her throat. She took a deep breath and walked on, ignoring the churning queasiness at the pit of her stomach. Seasickness was now a fact of life and, like everything in Chiara's life, she pushed it to the back of her mind and dealt with

the here and now. The future was too far away and too
erratic to think about.

Chapter Three

On another part of the ship, a young woman stood alone in a single beam of sunlight and stared into oblivion. Golden legs stretched out from a yellow sundress, her back braced against a salt-encrusted post.

"Stupid woman must be frozen," Chiara thought but then noticed the firm set of her jaw. "She's angry, no wonder she can't feel the cold." She stopped for a moment and watched as the woman uncrossed her legs and changed to a sitting position against the post, her bare feet now propped against the rail. Chiara had seen her around the ship, but she was always accompanied by a man in whom she was totally absorbed. Chiara doubted whether she would even recognize her.

She examined this woman carefully, taking special note of her features and tried to understand what a blue-eyed blonde was doing on an Italian migrant ship. She knew that many Northern Italians were blonde but there was something mysterious and strangely familiar about this

one. Scarlet-tipped fingers, holding a damp white hand-
kerchief with the name "AVA" delicately embroidered into
the corner, she wiped at her tear-streaked face, accentuat-
ing the most unusual nose that Chiara had ever seen. Not
unusual because of its size or shape but more so because of
the elegant 'Romanesque' structure on such an inelegant
face.

She could not help but stare, the exquisite finesse con-
trasted vividly with the sharp contours of her face and
the hollowed cheeks it was almost as if the nose had been
carved separately and placed there as an afterthought.
"Definitely not a peasant," she mused "more regal, like
someone from the aristocracy." For an instant, she thought
she must have said this out loud because the woman
turned and looked directly at her.

Chiara felt her hand drift to her own face. Her finger
slid silently down her nose as she contemplated her own
features yet again. Her nose felt huge as she rubbed her
finger up and down it. She felt what seemed like an enormous bump in the middle before it flared out and flattened
towards the nostrils. "No aristocratic finesse here," she
thought, "more like a gorilla or some sort of Neanderthal
caveman."

Compelled by the woman's aura of vulnerability,
Chiara slipped to her side.

At a closer inspection, she could survey the smoothness
of her skin and the silkiness of her hair, she realised that
the look of innocence was in fact due to her youth and
probably quite a large amount of inexperience. She was
maybe ten years older than Chiara but they seemed to be

worlds apart as they sat side by side. Finally, a light flickered in her dull reddened eyes. She felt the presence of Chiara and turned to face the child.

The tiny flicker of a smile died on her lips as she took in the scene beside her. A bedraggled gypsy-like child in a huge overcoat which was filthy from being dragged along the floor, equally filthy bare feet and a swathe of hair missing from the centre of her forehead.

She turned back to the ocean and contemplated leaving, but the child began to speak.

Although initially repulsed, she was soon enchanted. Chiara spoke little but she exuded a peaceful charisma which had an uplifting influence on Ava. "You know, there's a Romany saying where I come from," Chiara stated solemnly, "that you can walk away from the people you hate, but you can never walk away from yourself. You cannot run away and hide because you bring yourself along wherever you go. Learn to accept who you really are."

As she spoke, she kept staring at that same point on the horizon that had Ava's rapt attention. Ava's brow crinkled, "What on earth is this girl talking about?" she thought, "She is a child, and couldn't possibly know anything about me or my life." But of course, she did. As always, Chiara had summed up the situation and knew exactly what needed to be said, and as usual, she said it.

"See that ocean, it's full of fish, but just dangling a line over the edge won't catch any of them, will it?" she said.

Ava's attention had been piqued. She did not really understand, but was interested enough to find out what the child was talking about. She turned to face her and was

struck by the features of the girl. It was not so much that
the child was pretty, or even ugly, it was more that she was
struck by a sense of familiarity. She felt spiritually close to
her, yet they had never met. There was something in her
dark eyes. They contained so much knowledge. Her own
life was hidden in their chocolate depths.

It was as if this girl had always been a part of her existence. She blinked, and in a flash the vision was gone. The
girl was just a girl again; the sense of familiarity was gone.
The experience left her wanting to reach out to the child.
This little girl whom she had found repulsive could be
entrusted with her deepest secrets, her hopes and dreams,
and most of all, her intimate fears. From the change in
Ava's manner, Chiara was instantly aware that Ava had
experienced a flash of deja vu. For that second, she was Ava.
She could feel her pain and was spiritually in tune with
Ava's emotions.

Involuntarily, she reached out and touched the scarlet-tipped hand and enclosed it in her own. It was a simple
gesture that was profoundly intense. Two people became
as one and a lifetime of hurt and pain melted away. Ava
had grown in that instant, the little girl in her had dissi-
pated and Chiara, wise beyond measure, had transcended
to become a part of her inner soul. She had been given
her deeper insight which usually only comes with age and
experience.

She lifted her feet off the rail and brought them up, circling her knees with her arms. Turning her head around,
she was able to gaze at Chiara's features and assess them
more accurately. That acute feeling of kinship was no

longer there but she must trust this girl. "What did you mean when you talked about fishing?" she said.

Chiara turned her gaze to the ocean once again. Her eyes held a faraway look as she focused on a point on the horizon. She said, "When you dangle a line over the side of the boat, you won't catch anything, unless you put some bait on the end of it." Ava followed Chiara's gaze, looking out across the sea. Her brow wrinkled as if she was trying to understand the meaning of the message.

Chiara went on, "Unless the bait is something the fish likes to eat, it won't do much either. As well, there's all the other obstacles. Are the fish you want in the place where you're fishing? Are they hungry enough to take your bait? And if you're not catching anything, who's to say it's going to be any different tomorrow, or next week, or next year."

"Yes, I understand what you're saying but why are you telling me about fish?" asked Ava, who was bewildered by Chiara's words.

"Because life itself is like fishing," said Chiara. "What you want won't always be there. Occasionally, you need to look and sometimes you even need to give others what they want so they will take your bait in return."

"Do you mean bait a hook to trap what I want and reel it in to reap the benefits," she asked in a slightly disgusted tone.

"No, not that so much. What I mean is that life is give and take, you give, they take and then they give in return. Sometimes you are waiting forever. Even though you can see the fish around you, it's not possible to catch them immediately but if you are patient, eventually they will be yours. Do you understand?"

"I think so," Ava said softly. It was like their quarrel in the cabin, how she wants to have a baby now and Nico doesn't. "So, if I continue to use my desire as a bait, I will chase away what I am really after, the same as I would if I tried to catch a fish with a bait it didn't like."

"Something like that," Chiara replied, "I always find if I relate everything in life to nature, it all starts to make sense, because the grand scheme of things is based on a really simple philosophy."

"And what's that?"

" I haven't figured that one out yet."

"Well, do you know what I think it is?" Ava stated prophetically, inspired by her newly-acquired wisdom, "It is to be completely honest with ourselves and to treat others with the same respect we want to be shown."

"Also, that we take responsibility for ourselves at some point in our lives, " added Chiara.

"But don't we always?" Ava asked, a slight frown creasing her forehead.

"No!" stated Chiara emphatically, "I have seen so many people in Rome who spend their life blaming others for their mistakes. In the end, you find they were the ones who messed up somewhere by chasing pretend riches. These riches became so important that they covered their eyes to the other riches in life. They lost sight of what is important."

"That's pretty deep," Ava said, "It doesn't sound like something a girl your age would know about."

"No, actually it was a quote I borrowed from an old lady in Garibaldi Park. She spent most of her life feeding the pigeons. She told me how life is one long pathway and there are rocks scattered along it everywhere. She said we can either run blindly along and keep stumbling over them, or we can take our time and walk around them. Either way, she said, you cannot blame the rocks for being there. Even if you try to kick them out of the way, you will end up with bleeding feet.

Sooner or later, we must accept the rocks are there and be responsible for lifting our own feet and stepping over them. Some people never understand and keep stumbling, chasing dreams they don't need to make their life complete."

"Amazing! What you say is true. How did you gain so much wisdom? I mean, it's one thing to be told these things by the people around you but to understand them so deeply is entirely another, especially at your age," Ava asked perplexed.

"My parents had a street stall in Rome and, ever since I could walk, I've been living amongst the street people."

"But how could the people on the streets know so much about life?"

"Because they had to learn the hard way. The gypsies often roamed the streets and I made friends with a gypsy girl named Isabella. It was like we were destined to meet because she could almost read my mind. After I spent some time at the gypsy camp, I realised Isabella and I were two sides of the same coin."

"It sounds like she became a close friend?"

"More like a soulmate. Her parents were into witchcraft and black magic and all that stuff. It was a bit weird and I really didn't want to be a part of it, but they kept telling me I was the centre of their psychic energy. They kept repeating that Isabella and I would be soulmates forever, whatever that meant."

Chiara looked away. Ava heard a hint of reservation in her voice. "Will you have any family other than your parents in Australia" she asked.

"My parents have friends in Cairns," Chiara stated emphatically. "That's where we're headed."

"What about all this psychic stuff, will you continue with that when you get there?"

"I don't know, I doubt whether I have any psychic ability. All I know is that I'm able to understand people. I suppose I'll never know now because I don't think there are many gypsies in Australia."

"But do you really need gypsies?" Ava began but stopped short when she saw a familiar figure coming up the stairwell.

Chiara followed her eyes and looked back at Ava who had crossed her legs and was absently fidgeting with her wedding ring.

Taking this as her cue, Chiara whispered, "Don't forget, the answers aren't always in front of you, Ava." She stood up and slipped away quietly as Ava embraced her husband. Over his shoulder, she looked for the strange child who made such an impact on her. But she was nowhere to be seen. Then she remembered the girl's parting phrase, 'The answers aren't always in front of you,

Ava." She called me Ava, but how did she know, I never told her my name?

As she re-entered their cabin, Chiara knew she had discovered another soulmate. One to replace Isabella. But Ava was to be her soul-kin for life, not necessarily a soulmate. She would be in spirit. She and Ava were destined to be intertwined by a special bond. A gossamer thread which fate had selected to link the best part of their lives together. Each of them was the wing of a special butterfly, the centre of which would be the connection inspired by that single encounter on the boat trip to Australia in 1957.

Chapter Four

They drifted along the parched coastline. It was a wasteland compared to the northern Italian valleys which meandered like green snakes between snow-capped mountains or the foamy blue Mediterranean sparkling in the midday sun.

"I can't believe I actually agreed to come here," Ava whispered hoarsely, leaning her head against a pole. Nico drew heavily on the remnants of his cigarette, his eyes glazed as he stared across the glassy ocean. Smoke from his cigarette idly spiralled into the still hot air. He flicked the butt over the side and turned to face his bride. His eyes travelled across her shapely legs as they swung carelessly over the rail and upwards to her bare arms, bronzed, and shimmering in the sunlight.

Finally, his gaze fell upon her childlike face. She was deep in thought. Her expression was troubled. She looked at him as if she was no longer sure of the now gentle man before her. As he was about to speak, an unexpected wave tipped them sideways, knocking her off the rail and onto the deck. They stepped from one foot to the other, and clutched on to each other to regain their balance. The strong sea breeze tossed Ava's hair into golden wisps around her face.

"She looks like a baby doll," Nico mused, "so perfect, yet so fragile." All he needed was to dwell upon the rareness of her beauty, enjoy it without touching it and admire her loveliness. Even now, with what felt like a million miles between them and Italy, he melted with one glimpse of her delicate form. She possessed an intense magnetism and he often felt like pinching himself that she had agreed to become his wife. She was like a rare flower that bloomed in the centre of a garden filled with the most exquisite women in Italy.

They were together against all the odds which had included a pledge his father made about the woman who he personally selected to marry his son. The woman's family could provide ultimate power to the Palladino family. A union between them meant they would dominate the Tuscany wine growing industry and the Palladino name would become the most famous wine company in Northern Italy.

Power was the essence of being a Palladino. This wanton passion for power had fuelled his hatred for his family. The Palladino family was ruthless, destroying people and other families time and time again. Even acting with integrity and kindness could be viewed as a weakness, undermining the mighty Palladino dynasty.

He recalled how a servant was dismissed many years ago for chastising his sister, Rafaela, during a holiday in Naples. Rafaela refused to allow their servant to pay for an ice-cream which she had already taken and eaten from a mobile vendor.

In her usual arrogant way, Rafaela pronounced, "I am a Palladino," and that she was entitled to whatever she desired. Naturally, the vendor, a man who obviously derived his entire income from the stall, demanded payment. Rafaela related how the servant had gone against her orders and paid for the food and chastised her for being so selfish as to assume that, at eleven years of age, anything was hers for the taking.

The servant, who worked as a trusted chaperone to Nico and Rafaela, as well as to Nico's father and his two siblings during their childhood at the family villa, was immediately dismissed. He recalled how painful it had been to lose their beloved servant as he was the last link to his mother. Since she died, this servant was the only person to show compassion in a household filled with a lust for mastery and oppression.

Nico shook himself free from the painful trip back to an era he would rather forget. Adjusting his relaxed posture against the ship's rail, he reached across and tenderly lifted a lock of hair that strayed across his new wife's face. For a fleeting moment, as his fingers brushed her cheek, he felt the moisture of a renegade teardrop. When she blinked, he caught the hint of a tear glistening in the corner of her eye. He sighed deeply.

He wanted to console her but what could words offer? Any words would be meaningless because he had drawn the same conclusions as Ava - albeit secretly - that Australia was nothing like they imagined it would be. They were coming to a land that may not be fit for civilized Europeans to dwell in. Perhaps the trip had been a huge mistake. He could not console her with words because she would sense that he was covering up his true feelings.

He was racked with guilt for taking her so far away from her family. His thoughts were troubled, "We could have moved south or into another country in Europe," he pondered. "But I was insistent on Australia. It was my stubbornness, and there's nothing I can do about it now. I will have to live with it." Nico stopped himself from blurting out his regrets to Ava. He gazed into her beautiful eyes, "So young, so trusting. I have destroyed her innocence with false promises about the wonderful land we are going to."

No matter how hard he tried to escape from it, Nico still bore the Palladino trait that, to be a man, one must be strong, proud and able to make his own decisions, and formulate what he wanted out of life. He had used this trait as an act of defiance against his father's tyranny. It was now up to him, and him alone, to prove he was a man by showing he was strong and capable of surviving without the Palladino heritage as a prop.

To his way of thinking, the Palladino dynasty was a play in which they were all actors following a predetermined script which he could not accept. He wanted to break away and establish his own direction in life, rewriting the script to suit his own goals and ultimate mission.

Part of the break from his father's oppression included marrying the woman he chose and starting a life with her in the country of his choice, but he was beginning to question his motives for leaving Europe. Since they met, he never once questioned his choice of a partner but occasionally he silently admonished himself about his decision to start their married life in Australia.

Someone as perfect as Ava deserved more than he could offer without the Palladino millions to support them. He wanted to shower her with jewels and give her the luxury that only his father's estate could provide.

Even if they remained in Italy, a life of wealth and comfort was not possible. He had broken the arranged marriage plans, therefore he was no longer considered a true Palladino. As a consequence, he had to provide for his own wife and family. Unfortunately, his lifestyle meant he was ill-prepared to be the breadwinner.

How would he would be able to earn money in Australia? As humility did not come naturally to him, Nico found himself thinking about finding work as akin to grovelling like the beggars he would sometimes encounter on the city streets and to whom he would throw a few lire.

Nico was staring at Ava as if he was mesmerized. She reached up and touched his hand which was resting softly upon her cheek, "How the sun and sea have aged him," she mused as she studied his features, noticing the deep furrow between his brows. His dark complexion, usually young and supple, had acquired a leathery texture, stubble covered his lower face and neck, and deep lines had gathered around his eyes and mouth.

How much of his changed appearance was brought on by worrying about how they would make a new start. Even though he rarely spoke about their future, the tension in his face revealed how he feared what would become of them in Australia.

His once-shining ebony mane had flashed midnight blue in the sunshine. Now it hung in impotent ringlets around his face due to his many hours leaning over the rails, exposing himself to the unrelenting salt spray and strong sunlight. The blue-black sheen had gone and was replaced by a dirty rust-coloured highlight. Ava found it difficult to touch what she once found so smooth and indescribably masculine about her husband.

His eyes had not changed; they retained that piercing sensual quality which held her motionless in their powerful depth and intensity. His coal-black eyes were set in a brilliant white canvas and offset by luxuriant lashes which perfectly complemented a complexion of polished walnut.

She could not hold her tears back. She had buried them in a silent place, deep in her soul. Now they spilled out as her depression became all-consuming. "It will be better when we get there," she heard him say, although to her ears his words lacked conviction. Through her sobs, Ava saw her husband wipe a silent tear from his own cheek. His eyes met hers and were a mirror in which she glimpsed a bewildered young woman who vaguely resembled herself.

"She'll be better soon," he silently reassured himself, rolling another cigarette. He chanced another anxious glance before placing it between his lips and lighting it. Lowering the tobacco case to his pocket, he was transported back to the day his father placed the silver case in his hand almost 10 years ago. It was his twenty-first birthday. Much of his turbulent past was little more than a blur but not that night. It was as vivid as if it happened yesterday.

He saw his father's outstretched hand which he rarely reached out to Nico. He dropped the small silver case into his palm and enclosed his fingers upon it. "This was your great-grandfather's. Now you are a man, it is yours. May you pass it on to your son someday." It was a rite of passage: the eldest Palladino son always received the case when he proved himself to be a man.

He also knew that with the token silver case came the ultimate gift: the right to the legendary Palladino power, the vineyard estate, and the onus which came with the mighty Palladino title. It was these burdens which caused his bitter opposition. The oppressive Palladino title cost him his mother; it cost him a normal childhood and, most of all, it cost him the loving family he had always dreamed of. Instead, his father rarely spoke to him and his sister resented his existence. He could still see Rafaela's smile of victory as he left the family home for the very last time.

Returning to the present, he turned the case over in his palm to read again the inscription meticulously etched into the tarnished silver.

Nicenzio Alessandro Palladino II - 1867

He tucked it carefully into his pocket and resumed a slouching position over the ship's rail. His eyes again probed the desolate horizon. 'It will be better when we arrive,' he repeated in his mind. He was conscious that he was trying to convince himself that the trip was not a big mistake.

Was he a fool not to listen to his father and marry the woman agreed upon all those years ago? He could have kept his wife comfortably in Italy and started a family at the vineyard. A true Palladino would have embraced his succession as the head of the family. A Palladino proud of his heritage, that is!

He took his eyes away from the ocean and looked at the woman by his side. It all became crystal clear. Marrying Ava was the only choice; she was his destiny. Wherever they would go and whatever they would do, they would do it as a couple. He loved her more deeply than life itself. Whether it was in Italy or in a new country a world away, it would be with the woman he chose to have by his side until the end of eternity.

"When we reach Sydney, it will all turn out, you will see," he muttered. Ava turned to look at him, a frown on her forehead as she watched him blow a hefty stream of smoke from both nostrils.

Gina and Enzo were doing what had become a ritual. They stared blankly at the horizon from their cabin window as it cleared the wall of water each time the ship rolled on a wave. Although their gaze was now fixed on land rather than sea, their expressions remained unchanged. Their vigilant stance on either side of the porthole window still resembled sombre humanlike statues.

Daily rituals such as bathing and hair brushing were regarded as interruptions to their vigilance rather than basic grooming habits. They were performed as simply and as quickly as possible so they could again resume their positions at the window. They had lost hope that their long journey across the oceans would ever end. Within the tiny world of the ship, they were like automatons without care, hope or emotions.

Their daughter, Chiara, had not been present in the cabin for quite some time, and they didn't know where she was. Strangely, they were unconcerned about their missing daughter. In her absence, their vigil was uninterrupted. In their minds, her presence only created heartache, so maybe it was better that she was elsewhere.

The dry salt tang in the air and the crackling heat, which seared nostrils, was a perfect complement for the desolate sand dunes and bald rocks on the horizon. Beneath the jagged cliffs spanning the coastline were numerous tiny islands. As they sailed closer, they saw the islands which Chiara had been watching all day were not islands but rocky outcrops heavily stained with bird droppings.

When they were close enough to the shore to see above the sheer cliff faces, the land was barren, with no trace of trees or any other vegetation. The landscape did not change the entire time they cruised adjacent to the coastline. With land so close, bird life was plentiful and the occasional seagull would swoop down to grab morsels from the deck.

Some passengers often threw crumbs which encouraged more birds to settle upon the rails of the ship. Chiara watched them with half-hearted interest as they groomed themselves endlessly between having squabbles over food and roosting positions on the dropping-stained rails. Large pelicans also swam close by and occasionally landed on the deck, but, unlike the bold seagulls, they were wary of the passengers. The deck of the ship was the seagulls' domain and their constant squeals and squawks filled the air, overpowering the endless drone of the ship's motor.

Chapter Five

Breakfast was a lumpy mixture of oatmeal and another grain she could not identify. As usual, Chiara ate little, meaning she had plenty of leftovers she could feed the birds. Hopefully, she could entice a pelican to come closer. She really wanted to study this odd-looking bird.

Because the pelicans would not venture onto the deck, she threw lumps of the oatmeal overboard, hoping they would draw closer and scoop the food up in their massive beaks. Instead, the oatmeal lumps attracted an array of strange blue-finned angelfish which surfaced like sparkling jewels from the depths of the ocean. Their iridescent colours shimmered as they caught the sunlight.

Fascinated, she watched as the angelfish surfaced, lunged for the oatmeal, and dived back down again with their catch in their mouths. Like anything beautiful, they appeared and were gone again in quick succession. Soon, all that Chiara could see was the blue green water, so crystalline it might go down forever. She could not see any life, only clear watery depths, no bottom, and not even a ripple to indicate that seconds ago the sea was teeming with fish.

She wandered idly along the deck. Poker had long since lost its appeal and now she craved excitement of a different kind. As the boat was predominately a migrant transporter, it was not geared for entertainment. Chiara found her own ways of amusing herself. She continued walking slowly and barefoot along the deck, climbing the myriad of internal and external stairways that dotted all seven decks.

The fascination of discovering where they led had long since diminished; she knew every crevice on the public part of the ship intimately. Even the private areas and the ladders that led up to the bridge and down to the galleys were no longer exciting.

She easily outsmarted the staff by sneaking into the kitchen and grabbing a private stash long before the meals were served. Because she had beaten the rules, she no longer experienced the childish exhilaration which comes from being one step ahead of the adults.

The ship was more alive today. Many of the passengers were excitedly moving their hands and bodies. Their eyes and mouths were animated about something. It was not the usual droning conversations filling the atmosphere or all the morbid faces staring at the horizon. Today, there was a genuine excitement in the air. What was happening to lift their spirits?

She overheard a conversation about a place called Fremantle and another about coming into port soon. She deduced the ship was about to stop. Was this where they would disembark? Gina and Enzo did not mention anything to her but they rarely mentioned anything besides the necessary things. She wondered if they were nearly at Cairns. Could it be the voyage was almost at an end?

Her heart soared until she again gazed at the coast-line. Surely her new life could not be in that isolated wasteland? Certainly, her home in Rome with its con-crete monoliths and buildings opening directly onto the streets was equally arid but it was brought alive by a unique combination of historical pride and cultural em-pathy.

All along the streets, cafeterias were abuzz with laughter and conversation; little children played amid the piles of fruit and vegetables in their parent's stalls. All around, bright colours filled even the darkest corners.

The comforting aroma of tomatoes and garlic per-meated through the streets and alleys of Rome but here all she could smell was the salt tang of the sea. Nothing like home, there she understood the people and, most of all, the language. Here there was nothing: no houses to indicate life, no trees, or buildings, or sounds other than the constant squawking of the hungry seagulls.

No signs of civilisation. All the usual everyday things had been stripped away, leaving an emptiness. The land was desolate, an arid treeless desert. The jagged cliffs and crashing waves bore down on her with ominous intent.

Goosebumps spread over her arms and legs, and she trembled. An alien feeling of trepidation came over her as she returned to her parents' cabin. She found them staring at each other instead of through the window. For the Calvecchio family, Gina, Enzo, and Chiara, their first sightings of the west Australian coast that afternoon provoked deep anxiety.

Chiara was afraid. What would happen? How could they live in such a place? Her real fear of the unknown surfaced and made its way past her tough streetwise exterior into the sensitive recesses of her soul. It added to the state of flux into which she was drifting. The rest of the day passed quickly.

In the impending darkness, it was difficult to discern the size of the city. The heat was oppressive. To a travel-weary Ava, her first impressions of Freemantle were of a dirty place. The city was full of inhospitable closed doors attached to rusting tin shacks and rotted wooden buildings in dire need of repairs and a fresh coat of paint.

In this place named Fremantle, everything Nico and Ava saw disgusted them. Hotels were plentiful but in a pitiful state of repair with broken glass louvres. Shabby and tin roofed, the hotel buildings were the only premises with any form of life, but they were noisy, crowded, and full of dirty people too drunk to stand or just plain hostile and aggressive. A shiver of revulsion went through Ava; this type of vulgarity was unknown to her.

Dark-skinned Aborigines were plentiful. They congregated on the footpaths amongst filthy, unkempt sunburnt men who pushed their way through the dark skins and into the public bar where they spoke loudly and obnoxiously in a language neither Ava nor Nico understood.

Inside the hotels, the patrons spent a lot of time yelling at each other. Although the words were foreign, the inflection was obvious. They were not the frivolity and laughter one would hear in a bar in Italy.

Ava averted her eyes when she saw men staggering outdoors to spit on the dirty footpath or shout angrily at her fellow passengers as they walked past.

She walked with her head down and skirted around a repulsive patch of what looked like vomit on the footpath. The words were foreign, but one word being shouted frequently was "Wogs!" Although she had not heard it before and had no idea what it meant, she could tell it was a slur by the angry tone with which it was directed at them.

It was met with laughter and encouragement from the crowd inside the hotel, reinforcing that it was a universal term of abuse. The consensus seemed to be that migrants were not welcome, at least not by the Australians they had so far encountered.

Ava felt nauseous at the sights and stenches from the hotel and she was more than a little fearful of the crowds gathering on the streets around them. Their attention was focused on her and her lack of comprehension of what they were yelling added to her fear of what they wanted.

The jeers in her direction became nasty in their inflection and she cringed. She moved in closer to Nico as a circle of drunken men closed in around them.

"Hey, get a load of the pretty little wog girl," one very drunk young man yelled as he staggered toward Nico and Ava. A steady stream of saliva dribbled from his bottom lip like a baby who could not control his drooling. His eyes, although unfocussed, were riveted upon her. Ava's heart was thumping; her chest tightened and her breathing became ragged. All these men chasing them, surrounding them, shouting at them.

"Wanna have some fun, wog girl?" he belched, as his hand wiped the drool from his mouth. She clutched Nico's arm tighter. Her eyes were wide and terrified. 'What do they want?' she thought as the adrenaline coursed its way through her veins and she began to tremble.

Nico held her tight and forced her to continue walking while the youth kept staggering after them. "Hey, don't piss off yet!" he yelled as others cheered him from behind the hotel windows.

But she and Nico kept walking, increasing their pace until they were almost running. Ava's tight grip on Nico's arm almost cut off his circulation. As they approached the edge of the hotel, an arm landed on Nico's shoulder. In an instant, he was pulled away from Ava and into the alley beside the building.

Ava spun around, terrified now that Nico was no longer beside her. She felt like a rabbit that was about to be pounced on by a pack of wolves. Her heart thumped uncontrollably, as she looked around with panicked eyes for Nico. She froze as the overwhelming stench of stale beer and foul indecipherable odours invaded her nostrils.

"I asked ya if you wanted some fun, wog girl?" the man slurred from behind her. Another drunk lurched at Ava, pushing her off balance, manoeuvring her from the dimly-lit footpath into the dark alley where Nico was pinned against a wall. He was being savagely assaulted by several men.

She struggled against the attacker's grip. But even in his drunken state he was powerful and impossible for her to fight alone. Hot slobbering lips grated across her mouth, forcing her jaws open and cutting off her screams. She fought desperately against hands that groped her everywhere. Nico fought back, pushing against the arms restraining him but two others had joined in the attack and they pinned his arms behind his back. He could not move.

Another man had an arm around his neck, cutting off his ability to make any noise. They held him in a vice-like hold. The scene was bedlam: Ava was being sexually assaulted by a drunken stranger and Nico kicking his legs to escape the arms that restrained him.

Ava screamed and fought back against her attacker, her eyes wide with panic. But the more she struggled, the more he forced himself on her, becoming even more aggressive with his kisses and groping. Her screams came out as gurgles.

Moving around her neck and chest with his wet rubbery lips, leaving a trail of drool on her skin, she was finally able to scream, "Nico!" pounding her attacker with useless fists against his steel-hard back while the spectators at the side door to the alley cheered and coaxed him on. He attempted to push her against the wall and she kicked him. With his attention on restraining her legs and pushing himself against her to pin her to the wall, Ava was able to move her hands to the front of the man.

She raised her fist and hit him in the mouth as hard as she could. Blood trickled from where his teeth pierced his lip. He stopped momentarily to wipe the area. It was enough; Ava dragged a scarlet nail across his cheek gouging a deep track that made him bellow. He loosened his grip enough for her to wriggle free and run.

When the others realised she was getting away, the attention on Nico was momentarily forgotten. He managed to free one arm long enough to strike the leering face of his closest restrainer. Nico's strength and his hot Italian temper flared to the extreme as the heel of his shoe connected with the face of another attacker. As the man dropped to the ground, Nico turned on the others with a ferocity they could not compete with in their inebriated condition.

With bloodied noses and bruised faces, the men ran after the fleeing couple. Fortunately, the drunken men could not run fast but the words "Bloody wogs" echoed in the still hot air as Nico and Ava ran toward a crowd of boat passengers who were oblivious to what had happened.

A sobbing Ava was shaking with fear and delayed shock from the sheer brutality of the attack. Whatever she had expected of life in Australia, it was not this violation by what could only be described as a bunch of drunken savages. She was a decent married woman and she felt degraded. She had been treated far worse than a whore.

Surrounded by other Italians and with the strength and support of an equally disillusioned Nico, they made their way back to the ship, to the relative sanctuary of their spartan cabin. Ava scrubbed her face until it was almost raw and then remembering the nauseating stench of stale beer and the taste of her attacker's rubbery lips, she was overtaken by a sudden surge of sickness and heaved into the washbasin.

She was hollowed out, dishonoured, and that night even her husband's touch made her pull away. Her restless sleep was punctuated by fears that the attackers would somehow break through the cabin doors and finish what they had started. Nico could not sleep close to Ava and he spent the night on the floor in front of the door.

Ava had curled into a foetal ball on the bed and jumped every time she heard a creak or a noise in the corridor outside. Lulled by the gentle rocking of the ship against its moorings, Ava finally slipped into a restless sleep around 2:30 a.m. Even in sleep, she jerked in spasms as if she was attempting to remove her bruised soul from the taint of this hideous attack.

In the light of the day, the ordeal lost some of its horror but to Ava the sense of violation was still very real. To Nico, his pure and innocent wife was now soiled by the touch of another man. As much as he despised himself for thinking it, he could no longer look at Ava without thinking about her being assaulted. He could no longer see Ava without also seeing her being touched by someone other than himself.

After last night's incident, there was no way he would ever allow his wife to be exposed to the type of brutality she had suffered in Fremantle. Secretly, they both longed for the country they had left behind, for the security of knowing the language and the people and the comfort of being in a place they could call home.

Nico realized his power and title meant nothing here. He felt the sting of being made to feel inferior to other men. There was nothing he could do about it. They could not turn the boat around and return to Italy either, so he asked around for a quick way of earning extra money whilst they were berthed. Surely, he believed, Australia had more to offer than drunken louts and aggressive hostility.

Chapter Six

The ship was moored for three days and able-bodied men were sought to help with the stocking of rations. From early that afternoon to late at night, Nico ferried beef, pork and sheep carcasses to the cold rooms and lugged huge bags of rice, flour, oatmeal, and pasta into the ship's pantry. He literally fell into bed that night. He was exhausted from labour he was totally unaccustomed to and too tired to even attempt to embrace his still-shaken wife.

At dawn, he began the process all over again. His aching muscles screamed as he hauled hundreds of heavy sacks from the cargo hold to the workers waiting on the docks. He had little time to worry about Ava who spent the entire time in their cabin. He heard snippets of conversation around him that held traces of familiarity, especially when the term "wog" was used in reference to himself. Although still unclear of the meaning, it cut deep and he uttered a silent 'thank you' that Ava could not hear it.

Nico lifted a particularly heavy sack of grain, his muscles bulging, and the pain shooting across his shoulders. He made his way to a group of workers on the far end of the wharf. It was the voices that caught his attention, then his head whipped up and he forgot the pain in his back. With newfound strength, he threw the sack onto the pallet at their feet. His eyes blazed like black onyx as he glared openly at their faces.

Contemptuous bile rose in his throat as he recognised some of them. One man turned and grinned at him exposing the deep gouge etched into his cheek. The throbbing vein at his temple threatened to explode. The man pointed to the rest of the sacks near the boat then to the pallet before turning and spitting into the dirty water beside him. He did not show a hint of recognition from two nights ago, but Nico certainly recognised him, as well as several of the other attackers.

He continued to stare as he clenched and unclenched his fists, the muscles in his jaw twitching as he gritted his teeth in defiance. "Oy wog," the man with the wounded face yelled from the end of the wharf, "Get the bloody sacks, eh!" He reinforced his demand by again pointing at the sacks and the pallet. But Nico remained rigid, even as the man walked back towards him; he kept clenching his fist into a tight hard ball as the man came closer and closer.

"I said the sacks, wog," the man growled as he spat onto the timber, just missing Nico's feet. Nico fought the impulse to slam his fist into the man's face. Even in sobriety, his arrogance was menacing but Nico kept a lid on his simmering fury.

The urge to lash out and damage the other cheek was powerful and he was a proud man who did not turn away from such injustice. "I should kill you," he hissed in Italian. The man continued to stare at him with hostility, not comprehending Nico's words and not showing any glimmer of recognition, let alone remorse. Nico hated that he could not speak the language well enough to give this thug a piece of his mind. He could only curse him in Italian which resulted in him being ridiculed by the attacker's supporters in the crowd.

As much as he wanted to lash out, he knew that to do so would be futile if none of them knew what the attack was about. He would simply be branded as another troublemaking "wog" and he had been here long enough to realise that a troublemaking wog had little chance of gaining employment anywhere once the word got around. In the standoff, he felt totally emasculated, impotent and weak.

At that moment, Ava's face flashed before him. He and Ava were 'the strangers' and he realised what it was to be a wog. His eyes dropped, he lifted a hand to his sweaty brow and pushed back a lock of his thick black hair, running his fingers through it, and pulling it harshly away from his scalp thus releasing the tension in his jaws. He pivoted sharply on his heel and stalked towards the boat for more sacks. With each step, he felt another piece of eroded morale crumble from his proud shoulders.

He justified the pain from the work as being his punishment for not seeking justice against this man for what he had done to Ava. His beautiful wife, he loved her, yet he could not fight for her and the humiliation was worse than any pain he felt now, any pain he had felt in the past and far more humiliating than having to face his father.

The rest of the day was uneventful. He continued to work without acknowledging his tormentor's presence again and justified his backing down as being the means of paying for his and Ava's continued journey away from this hostile town. In the back of his mind, he was toying with the idea they may need to return to Italy. His spirit for the moment was broken, his faith in Australia shattered by this town's vicious inhabitants.

So far as he knew, Freemantle was a part of a larger hostile country. In his mind's eye he contemplated that the time may come when he would have to concede his mistake to his father and accept that his powerful family would eternally dominate him.

But he wasn't ready to concede defeat and confront the possibility that he was wrong. Could they ever live as a couple in Australia and retain their dignity? But what was eternally worse was that one day he may be forced to return to the vineyard like a wounded dog with its tail between its legs. But would being humble to his father be any less bearable?

Either way, his pride was strong, he would stand against the arrogance and hostility that surrounded him here, but he knew he could never stand the humiliation of standing before his family as a failed man. This was the moment when he decided he would never ask his father for assistance to return. Somehow, he would make a life for Ava and him in Australia.

Chiara delighted to be investigating the streets. They were not so different to Rome after all, she mused. Perhaps the buildings were a little more dilapidated and the architecture vastly different and the searing heat from the cement against her bare feet was worse, but she discovered that the people really were much the same.

The faces were different, the language was different, but the laughter in their eyes and the tone of their voices as they gathered together and talked reminded her of the way Italians communicated. There were the crusty old men who sat in the gutters, or on the steps of houses and hotels, the mothers who yelled at their children from open windows, the creaking park swings and the cars that billowed dust everywhere as they roared along the streets.

One thing that was almost identical was how, as she walked, she was invisible. She was still the tough street kid walking on the edge of life's pathway, enclosed in her own private shell which nobody took the time to investigate. Not here and not in Italy. Somehow, deep inside, she knew she would always be encased in this shell but she didn't want it to be broken which would be akin to being smothered by the very thing she fervently pushed aside.

She loved and hated the solitude at the same time. In her shell, she was safe from the pressures of society that always frowned upon the different, safe from the hurt that came with loving, but most of all she was safe from herself. The one person she despised more than anyone was herself, the tough withering creature who showed nothing of herself but scorn and contempt.

Lost in her musings, she almost missed the single blade of grass that poked its head through a crack in the concrete. It was growing wild amidst the harshest environment. Even though it was alone in the grey expanse, like her, it was growing where it wanted to be, not where it had been planted. It survived by its own wits, found its own nourishment and was alone and content in its isolation. A tiny speck of green on a hard grey slab and, if someone trod on it, it was only crushed temporarily because its roots were sturdy enough to spring back and regenerate.

"Yes," she thought, "people and nature really are the same, if only others took the time to see themselves in nature, maybe they wouldn't waste so much of their lives regretting the past or fearing the future." She bent down and plucked at the grass, only succeeding in breaking off the exposed blade. She smiled; next week it would be back again as green and strong as ever because, like her, the real strength was hidden beneath the surface

She found out that Cairns was still a long distance away. Chiara hoped it would be as open and free as she had found Fremantle to be. The sun-baked arid plains allowed her to bask in her own isolation without having to seek isolation. She could witness the hostility of families without needing to be hostile herself and she could revel in the solitude and take her time simply to appreciate everything that surrounded her without feeling that claustrophobic closeness of others.

She was happy that she had not lost the freedom to be whomever and whatever she wanted to be. Her only obligation was to herself which suited her just fine for she had breathed in the dusty landscape and came to understand the fragile power of all that surrounded her.

The final voyage to Sydney was filled with anticipation. The migrants who did not stay in Western Australia were anxiously preparing for the imminent start to their new lives away from the ship.

For Nico, the final leg of the voyage was filled with trepidation and fears for the future although for Ava it was all an anxious blur. She rarely ventured from the cabin and never without her husband by her side. She had become a wild-eyed woman-child who was frightened to be alone and terrified about what the future held.

After a week, the desolate landscape became greener and fresh hope surged within the small migrant ship community.

Chiara already had a vision of her new home. Fuelled by snippets of conversation she overheard, she imagined wild forests and mountains, waterfalls and rocky cliffs covered in ferns and mosses. Her vision, however, was drawn from a great empathy she had with the land. The surroundings she imagined reflected her bond with nature - her wild and free spirit that knew no bounds – her feelings went far deeper than her need to live within the aesthetics of the surroundings. She became lost in her dreams.

Chapter Seven

For Gina and Enzo, the trip to Sydney was simply more of the endless sameness, of day after day standing at the porthole window, staring. All their dreams, all their possessions, all their friends were in the haze of the past. Their homeland, the streets they loved had become a dangerous places. They would never be able to walk freely through Rome ever again. Freedom and sanctuary meant no dreams, no hopes, no visions. Just a life where they would be safe even if it was a life without a soul. Safe from fear, betrayal, hatred, evil, and safe from the monsters who would kill them all in a heartbeat to protect the secrets they carried with them.

They could start again; they were indifferent for themselves. But for Chiara, they were determined she must never know. She must be free to enjoy this new world and make a life. They never wanted her to feel the fear of always keeping secrets. Always hiding. To never feel proud of being a Calvecchio. To be frightened that one day she would also feel the horror of knowing her name would be a mark of shame and fear. Her world must be clean and protected from all the debris her father left behind on the streets of Rome.

"Arrivederci, our beloved Italy, our new life is about to begin."

In their minds, Australia was a colonial frontier, a wild forgotten country. Foreign people and foreign foods. No ancient buildings and cobbled streets like Rome with a history spanning back to their forefathers. This country was an untamed wilderness and they were about to disappear into it.

There was no excitement, no fanfare when they boarded, nobody to bid them bon voyage – only a calm, sad acceptance as they felt their souls drip away into that vast ocean outside their porthole.

Finally, when the ship reached Sydney, Chiara was able to view her surroundings. Far from being the desolate outpost she expected, Sydney turned out to be a bustling, chaotic city filled with wide streets and strange cars. The language was foreign and she struggled to understand the chatter around her but her parents seemed to know where they were going.

To Chiara, it was all very exciting, People walked in unform lines. Well-dressed women and stylish men with strange hats jostled each other at the street crossings. The chatter was constant and she wished she could understand a little of it. She had so many questions, everything was different and she wondered where the gypsies were, or if they even existed. They were everywhere in Rome selling their wares, professing their magic but here they proved elusive.

They walked from the boat to the train station amidst the chaos of finding their way through the foreign city. The bustle reminded Chiara of a colony of ants and she giggled at how they all walked with purpose towards an undisclosed destination.

Standing on the platform, Chiara watched wide eyed as people hurried back and forth, some with mountains of luggage, others with only a duffel bag or an official-looking briefcase in their hands.

Everybody was in a hurry. She wondered what was so important that they all needed to rush around so much.

Finally, the train doors slid open and the Calvecchio family found their seats and settled in for the long trip north.

The whistle blew and the train chugged into motion, another adventure, and more corridors to explore for Chiara. But for Gina and Enzo, the carriage windows may as well have been portholes and the trees and land simply more glassy water. They assumed the same positions, either side of the window, staring blankly outside. Chiara doubted whether they even noticed the changing landscape which slipped by as the train followed the rails north

When the train came into Brisbane, Chiara was disappointed to learn that Cairns was still many days of travelling north. For two weeks in Brisbane, they stayed in a wooden shack at the migrant centre.

Besides leaving to bathe and eat, Gina and Enzo would rarely venture out. They were wary of their fellow Italians and did not want to draw any attention to themselves by becoming social.

Chiara, on the other hand, used the time to explore her new surroundings. She knew it was only temporary but she enjoyed all her discoveries like the massive mulberry tree that she could climb with other children, picking the delicious berries that stained everything a deep purple.

All too soon, they were boarding another train for Cairns, their final destination and the start of their new life in Australia.

"The journey will soon be over," Chiara mused after the second day on the rattling noisy train, but really her journey was only beginning.

The trip was punctuated by night and day but Chiara remembered every town, every stop, every new tree, and every strange animal she saw along the way. She could hardly believe the animals. She saw the hopping kangaroos and enormous birds called emus. An emu ran alongside the train as if it was in a race with the carriages. For a while, the emu was even winning the race.

She felt a pang of homesickness as she caught glimpses of ocean along the way and she secretly hoped that the ocean would be close in Cairns. After six weeks, the rolling ocean had become her friend. The people, the birdlife, the fish: they all filled her days with wonder and amazement. Amazement at how big the world was and how much water separated her homeland from her new land.

The grass was high alongside the tracks. Tiny seed heads sprouted as they shone dusty pink in the afternoon sun and the birds were plentiful. She watched flocks of white cockatoos with their strange yellow tufts and the never-ending sea of grey and pink parrots, such comical looking birds. 'Galahs,' someone said as they pointed to them and Chiara tried to repeat the strange word, giggling as she stumbled over it. Learning English was going to be challenging but fun. It seemed like such a pretty language and she could not wait until she was able to speak freely with people other than her parents.

The plains were green, like ripe olive groves and the further north they travelled, the greener the land became.

Grassy plains gave way to salt pans which were an endless sea of white arid baked earth. The unforgiving heat reflected and danced in the distance like a strange expanse of nothingness which put on a performance of waves on the horizon. Just as suddenly, they plunged into shadowy tree-filled forests and emerged where kangaroos were plentiful. The mothers proudly showed off their babies in their pouches as they grazed on the long grass beside the tracks. She stared at the horizon, amazed at the way it swayed in the heat making the tracks ahead appear buckled and warped.

The patches of green again disappeared into more dry saltpans, followed by baked brown earth and back into dense rich greenery. The train pulled its way up steep inclines towards the mountains as the sun started its slow descent to the horizon. The sight of the thick misty forest in the dusky light filled Chiara with longing as she watched it slip silently past.

As the day gradually darkened, gentle rain misted the windows. Chiara squinted as a final shaft of sunlight penetrated the canopy and shone into her eyes. She watched the brilliant orange ball disappear under the red and pink streaks of a tropical sunset as they left the mountains behind and continued the ever-changing journey north.

After staring at the darkening horizon for what seemed an eternity, Chiara fell into a restless sleep. She dreamed of being lost in an arid dusty land but not being scared. She dreamed of being carried in the claws of a giant eagle and dropped onto a soft bed in the rainforest and feeling the wet dew as she lay in the roots of a massive tree. She dreamed of fairies and goblins with the characters of her fairytales coming to life and leading her to an unknown destination. She dreamt of unfamiliar scents and a strange softness.

When she woke beside her father, her head resting on his shoulder, she thought the carriage was also a part of her dream. It did not take long for her to remember this was not her bedroom in Italy, this was not even the boat they had spent six weeks on. This was a train and she was travelling with her parents; she was in a strange country where they spoke a different language and there was an adventure waiting for her at the end of the journey. With that thought she nestled, smiling contentedly, onto her father's shoulder and drifted back into blissful slumber.

Night blended into day, until finally they arrived at their destination.

There was a cacophony of noise and smoke from the train when they disembarked. People Chiara had never met before but who spoke Italian greeted her parents at the station. They drove them to their home which was a large sprawling highset timber house in a grove of trees dripping with small, yellow delicious-looking fruits.

"Go ahead, you can eat them. They are called mangoes," the man said, as he plucked one and handed it to Chiara.

She looked at it, puzzled, and bit into the skin.

They all laughed. The man took the mango and peeled the skin back revealing a deep yellow flesh that dripped succulent juicy nectar and smelt like something the ancient gods had delivered. Chiara was in heaven! She plucked another, and another until her arms were full.

She followed the others up the long winding staircase onto the widest verandah she had ever seen, depositing her stash of mangoes onto a long table. At intervals along the verandah, huge slouched armchairs were positioned to overlook the lush forest beyond.

Chiara was not privy to the hushed conversations inside between them and her parents, nor did she care. All she wanted was to be able to explore this hot, tropical wilderness she would now call home. The sooner the better, she thought, as she peeled back the skin on another juicy mango. Her parents emerged from the house and they were taken to a tiny weather-beaten cottage down the path beyond the mango trees.

Although she had little in the way of possessions in Italy, and was accustomed to the gypsy ways and life on the streets, Chiara was repulsed by the room she was standing in.

The body odours of past residents permeated the mattress. The smell was disgusting. It mingled with the sour odour coming from the layers of mildew on the walls and ceiling.

The one window opposite the heavy timber door was coated in so much grime that the sunlight barely filtered through. The light inside the cottage was so dismal that it appeared to be early dusk instead of late afternoon. The paint on the ceiling was blistered and peeling and large cobwebs hung precariously over her bed.

She stood on her toes and looked out. The thought came to her, 'Why did we end up here? We all loved Italy, life was good.' Slowly, Chiara started to put some pieces of the puzzle together. Could her parents be running away from something? Was that why this tiny dusty unpainted room with three beds, a wardrobe, a filthy sink and one window was to be their home?

The other buildings appeared to be in an equal state of neglect and disrepair. She looked at her parents questioningly. The filthy cottage reminded her of the way the gypsies lived, except their homes were often relocated when the authorities decided it was time to move them on.

She turned on the tap for a drink but thought better of it when the water was an orange colour. When she tried to open the window, the latch came off in her hand. Thankfully, a breeze wafted in though the open doorway. A crack between the roof and the walls afforded some unintended ventilation but very little in the way of extra light.

Chiara was overwhelmed. She looked at the silhouette of her parents sitting at the table with some new people who had arrived several hours ago. These strangers seemed more formal and were dressed in suits which made them look official. They were all deep in a very animated discussion and she wondered what was going to happen to them. The impact of that reality was enormous. There was so much to get her head around.

She was silent and could not speak as she sat down outside against the dusty door frame. Clutching her knees, she buried her face against them. For the first time since leaving Italy, she began to weep.

She cried not for the country she would never see again, not for the stinking room she had been brought into, not even because of the blowflies buzzing around her sweaty body. She cried because she recognised that she had a weakness - this weakness was fear, and she despised herself for it.

Chapter Eight

Sydney had been a merry-go-round of factory jobs for Nico, labouring on the wharves and even gutting fish at a local seafood restaurant but, no matter where they went, they came up against the same prejudice they encountered in Fremantle.

Ava was still afraid to leave their room alone. Even though they shared the boarding house with other new Australians, she did not trust them enough to attempt a friendship.

There was an interesting mixture of cultures in the boarding house. A Hungarian couple of similar ages to her and Nico, a French couple with two children, three single Dutch men and an older Spanish woman she suspected was a prostitute as she received many visitors late at night and sometimes she left alone and brought men home with her.

None ever stayed long and Ava had grown used to the sound of the door across the hall opening and closing at all hours of the day and night, their hushed voices and giggling in the hallway as they entered her room and the almost silent footsteps as they left several hours later.

Aside from the fact she saw them in the corridor as they went to the shared toilet and bathroom facilities, Ava kept to herself. Having a conversation was difficult because of all the different languages. Anyway, she did not wish to get close to anyone. Through a side window, she could see a tiny yard where the French children played.

There was a large communal lounge area downstairs and occasionally she could hear the Dutch men laughing and drinking and obviously having a good time, or the French man tinkering on the old piano. He was a very good pianist and she found the tunes he played were soothing.

Still, she continued to stay inside in the upstairs room almost all day, looking out the front window, searching the street for Nico, waiting for him to come home so she did not feel so alone. She had become so desperately withdrawn and depressed that it was not uncommon for her cheeks to be wet with tears. Since Freemantle, Ava's only emotions were sadness and fear.

It was a long time since she had laughed. Nico tried to make her laugh by telling her about amusing things he had learned at work. His English was becoming quite good. He was beginning to form friendships and could have conversations with the other people in the building without too much difficulty.

Although he and Ava didn't speak English inside their room, he tried to teach her a few words, pleading with her to accompany him downstairs to mingle with the other residents. Always she refused. As a result, Ava still had very little grasp of the English language.

She longed to have the courage to enter the street and explore the shops while Nico was at work but was terrified of being assaulted again. She remained traumatised by what happened in Fremantle. She sat and waited in the safety of the room, behind the glass window where she could watch the activities in the busy street below.

Some afternoons, they ventured out together to do chores, to buy groceries, especially tomatoes, garlic and fresh herbs as Ava had become quite adept at simple pasta dishes. They were reminders from her days with her mother & her Nonna and the happy evenings at the kitchen table with her family.

Her brothers talked and laughed about their day at school and helped their father in the afternoons at the Palladino vineyard where he worked. Her mother talked about the other women in the village while her father got happily merry on red wine and smoked his thick Italian cigars.

Her father had worked in the Palladino vineyards since before she was born and they lived in the village adjacent to the vast estate. Now she pondered for hours as to whether she had destroyed her family's lives by eloping with Nico which only made her depression and self-loathing worse. Cooking and preparing meals was her one joy.

She knew her meals were not yet as good as what her mother made in Italy but they were certainly passable. Nico never let on that her pasta was nowhere near the standard of their cook; he ate with relish and told her how delicious it was. He could see that cooking was the one thing that gave her life meaning. She often experimented with new recipes from the book her mother had given her before she married.

Her 23rd birthday came and went without any event except a small party downstairs that her husband persuaded her to attend. There was a card from her parents and a silver pendant with an Australian opal from her husband.

The other residents tried to befriend her, offered her a drink and the French man played some party tunes on the piano but Ava continued to keep herself isolated. She refused to laugh or dance with the others or her husband or to try her hand at the piano. Nico tried to coax her into it, knowing she was actually an accomplished pianist. She detested Australia, detested the depression that was destroying her soul and was beginning to resent Nico for bringing her to live in this hellhole. Sydney was not the city or the life she had hoped for.

When she first started feeling ill and began throwing up every time she smelt any type of odour, Ava assumed it was caused by the stress of her reclusive lifestyle. She lost a lot of weight. Her periods had stopped months ago. She had always been agreeable, but now she was constantly arguing with her husband. She could not hold down any morsel of food. As soon as she rose from the bed, she became nauseous, even when her stomach was completely empty.

At first, she was not overly concerned, but when it persisted for several weeks, she began to worry it may be more serious. Nico was more and more concerned as each day passed and she became thinner and her complexion paler. "Ava, I don't care what you say. Look at you, you are weak and pale and everything you eat comes up again," said Nico angrily after another one of their regular arguments, "I am taking you to a doctor."

Ava glared at him, "I don't need a doctor, the doctors in Australia will be the same as everyone else. Don't you understand, to them we are only migrants, they won't care." She knew she was being irrational but couldn't help it. She often succumbed to bouts of melancholy these days and it was not unusual for her to dissolve into tears over nothing.

So, this time when she began to cry Nico sat patiently opposite her and said, "The Hungarians downstairs told me there is a clinic not far away that has an Italian doctor so I have already made an appointment for tomorrow afternoon."

Ava looked at him indignantly through her tears; she could not believe he would do that without telling her first. She was about to tell him so when a sudden burst of nausea caught her by surprise. She had just enough time to run through the door and into the shared toilet.

When she returned, Nico was still sitting on the same chair and he calmly repeated, "I will be home at four tomorrow, be ready and we'll walk to the doctors and find out why you are sick all the time."

She pouted like an insolent child, but obediently allowed Nico to put her into bed and draw the covers over her thin, pale body. She was too weak and ill to argue any more. She drifted into a troubled sleep.

Nico sat for a long time in the chair beside the bed watching her thin chest rise and fall, her beautiful face, pale and ashen, the cheeks hollowed. Her hair, once so luxurious and silken, lay limply around her bony shoulders.

"What is happening to us, Ava?" he whispered to his sleeping wife. He closed his eyes and leaned back in the chair pressing both his hands against his temples, sighing softly.

He felt defeated as he thought about how it had been when they first met and how she had drawn away from him. Day by day, he watched her becoming more distant. He did what he often found himself doing these nights, alone in that same chair, scouring his mind for a way to bring a tiny glimmer of happiness to his wife's face.

His shoulders slumped, he had tried everything imaginable; but nothing had any effect. She had become so despondent that even he could not lift her spirits. Slowly, he rose from the seat and quietly slid into the bed beside her, longing to feel her warm body against his once again, her breath sweet and comforting as she slept in his arms like she used to.

He attempted to embrace her sleeping body, only to feel the pain of rejection as she rolled to her other side and moved closer to the edge of the bed. He dreaded what the doctor would say tomorrow. He was restless and sleepless until, finally, he fell into a fitful sleep.

Chapter Nine

Nico and Ava sat in the doctor's office a week after the first visit, anxiously waiting on the results of Ava's blood tests. The doctor entered with a massive grin on his face. "Congratulations," was all he said.

Nico and Ava were bewildered.

He pointed to the word on the report: "Pregnant." Nico and Ava were trying to take it in. Neither Ava nor Nico had considered the possibility of Ava being pregnant as the reason for her illness. Their sex life had become so scanty that it was almost non-existent these days.

"Yes, she is definitely pregnant" the doctor assured them after Nico asked him for the third time. He shook his head in disbelief and stared at his astonished wife. After having a chat about nutrition and some medication to help with the morning sickness, they walked out in a blissful haze of disbelief.

Later that night, Nico noticed that a shine had returned to Ava's eyes. It was like a veil had been lifted. The Ava he had fallen in love with was slowly emerging from a deep dark cavern within.

She had cooked a minestrone and even attempted to eat a bowlful herself although this time when she rushed for the toilet, she felt elated instead of drained, knowing the reason for her nausea was because a child was growing inside her. The child she had secretly wished and hoped for since her first meeting with Nico on the school excursion to the winery where the grapes her father so lovingly cared for in the vineyards were turned into a delicious wine.

A spark had been lit inside her and she began to feel alive again.

A week later, after the news went around the boarding house that they were expecting, Ava found herself deluged with baby clothes and advice on pregnancy. The women of the house were knocking on her door and she was joining them in their rooms during the day and occasionally in the lounge downstairs at night. Her English was rapidly improving and she felt a kind of mellowness she had never experienced before.

She realised these people were friends and that Australia and its people were not all like her experience in Fremantle. Life was beginning to have meaning again. Gentle laughter and a depth of feeling for Nico that she never thought possible rapidly replaced her depression. He too felt that his Ava was returning, she was coming to life again. She allowed him to embrace her and touch her although they both were very cautious about lovemaking in case it could in some way harm the baby.

Tonight, they were eating dinner, a chicken dish, with the French family in the lounge downstairs. Jacques and Nico were sharing a cigar while Ava and Madeleine played a board game with the children. When they finished, Pierre, the couple's youngest child, moved to the piano and attempted to play a tune. It was a tune Ava knew well and had often played with her brothers when they were children. She sat beside Pierre and with a smile she proceeded to play a complementary tune which enhanced the boy's playing.

When they finished, they were surrounded by applause, not only from Jacques, Madeleine, and Nico but also from the Dutch men who had entered the room. Pierre was beaming. He had never sounded so good and wrapped his little arms around Ava and gave her a kiss on the cheek. She surprised herself by responding to his childish embrace with tears of joy at feeling like she had been accepted.

That moment was a turning point. The rest of the evening was filled with laughter and dancing. When she joined her husband in a slow dance as Jacques played, she felt as if her life could never be more complete than it was at that very moment in the arms of the man she loved.

It was not long before she ventured out of the house, sometimes alone and at other times in the company of the wives who lived in the house.

They wandered for miles, sometimes catching buses into the city to look at clothing. Other times, they wandered through the large department stores trying expensive perfumes, not caring that they could not afford to buy them. Ava laughed when at one counter she tried a nail polish and ended up with four different colours on one hand. She went on to sample the huge array of cosmetics from bright pink to a blood red lipstick.

Marta helped her select patterns and fabric for maternity clothes and explained that her trade in Hungary was dressmaking. Ava made a mental note to ask Nico for a sewing machine so she could make clothing for herself and the baby. They stopped for a lunch of fish and chips and strolled down to the riverside to eat in the park. She was amazed at the pigeons flocking around for the crumbs the women were throwing.

She was now almost at the halfway point of her pregnancy and was beginning to swell noticeably. Within weeks, Ava put the weight back on that she had lost. She was so happy that Nico could not believe how she shone. Her skin glowed with a radiance of its own. Nico revelled in her joyful transformation.

She felt exhilaration as she began sorting through baby furniture and exploring the toy departments. Her friends were as excited about the new arrival as Ava, and even Nico was surprised at how he began to look forward to becoming a father.

He surprised her one afternoon with a pram that he bought from a colleague at work. He had pushed it all the way home and, with each step, he realised more and more how much he was going to enjoy being a father. And who better to be the mother of his child than Ava who would be a wonderful mother. In his mind, he had already selected names, none of them being Nico Palladino IV.

No, he had something much stronger in mind – something that did not reflect his heritage or remind him of his family.

Ava liked the name Angelo, but it was not what Nico had in mind. The name he chose was a secret which he would not reveal until his son was born.

"What if it's a girl?" Ava laughed.

"I'm certain it's a boy," he replied although they both knew a daughter would be equally loved and welcomed into the family. However, Nico secretly wished that his firstborn would be a son.

Marta and Madeleine also had names selected and they only referred to the baby by those names. Somehow, Nico could not imagine a son of his being called Michel or Grigor Palladino. With the prospect of a baby, Nico and Ava put aside their resentment about Australia and began to accept that it was where their future would be.

Together they wrote of the happy news to their families in Italy. Ava knew her parents would be ecstatic. She imagined her mother would begin knitting as soon as the letter had been read, however Nico was a little perturbed by the knowledge that his father would not be so gracious.

"Maybe one day, when my father is an old man, he may want to know his grandchildren," he thought to himself although he cried a silent tear knowing that this would probably never happen and that his son would never know a grandfather's love from Nico's side of the family.

"Not to worry," he thought, "our children will have more than enough love from Ava and myself, and besides.... look at all the aunties and uncles our baby will have right here in Australia. Who needs the Palladinos anyway," he chuckled to himself. He felt pride that their life in Australia was beginning to show a future filled with happiness and contentment. "I don't need the vineyard, or the power, or my father," he said aloud to himself.

Ava was well into her fourth month of pregnancy with an obvious bulge and beginning to feel tiny fluttering movements inside her.

She was ecstatic, the morning sickness had long passed and everything so far was just fine, according to her doctor.

That was why she ignored the tiny cramps while walking home with a bag of groceries one afternoon. Nico was due home in a few hours and she wanted to surprise him with his favourite pasta dish although she was a little disappointed that she couldn't find fresh oregano at the greengrocers. She would have to use dried instead.

When she was almost home, an agonising pain went through her lower back. She had to sit still for a couple of minutes on the bus seat waiting for it to pass before getting up and walking towards the boarding house. As she climbed the inside staircase, she tripped and the pain turned into another spasm. She lifted herself off the floor and sat cradling her stomach until the spasm passed.

She knocked on Marta's door when she reached the hallway. There was no answer as another blinding spasm began. She tried the Spanish woman's door, she had never associated much with her in the past. All she heard from inside was an aggravated male voice.

By this stage, Ava was in so much pain she could barely walk. She looked at the stairs, she knew it would not be possible to go down them again so she walked the few excruciating steps to her own front door. Nico would be home soon.

As she reached their door, she felt an extraordinary sensation of pushing. Ava couldn't remember much from that moment. She was vaguely aware of entering their room and collapsing on the bed, the pains were ripping her insides apart.

She passed out amidst searing pain which was how Nico found her later that afternoon. Almost comatose, her skin tinged blue and lying on their bed in a pool of her own blood. A tiny foetus no bigger than a newborn puppy lay lifeless between her blood-smeared legs. Ava was too weak to speak; it would not have been possible for her to call for help.

Contrary to what he had told Ava when she had desperately expressed her desire for a child, Nico was a changed man. He was looking forward to becoming a father so when he saw the lifeless form of his first son on that bed, he felt as if a part of him had died with that child. Nico had never felt more helpless in his entire life.

Chapter Ten

Three days after her fifteenth birthday , Chiara started her first period. She was a woman now, and it frightened her. It was not so much the blood; she had been expecting that for years, in fact she was the only one in her class who had not started. The girls in her class talked of nothing else.

What frightened her was that now she needed to conform to what society expected of her. She could no longer be the tearaway Italian gypsy child; she could not even use her assumed innocence as a scapegoat for her actions. She was a woman and with this change came adult responsibilities.

She walked solemnly past the tangle of vines that covered the back entrance to their little green dilapidated cottage. Sitting on the step, she surveyed the maze of coconut and mango trees around her. The tropical passionfruit hung like large golden globes from the laundry roof.

Her father purchased the tiny timber cottage last year from the people who had assisted with their arrival and he and Gina were slowly making improvements. A railway line ran behind the unkempt back yard and the neighbourhood children played on either side. Although it was humble and small, it was becoming a real home.

But the thought of the delicious fruit did not tempt her at this moment when her life, as she knew it, was changing. The house was clean and tidy but too crowded even though it was only the three of them. Chiara heard her mother clattering around in the kitchen preparing the evening meal and decided not to go inside. She and her mother could never speak to each other civilly. She was not about to tell her what was happening to her body.

She pulled her bicycle out from where it was propped against the side of the house, "Where are you going?" her mother demanded angrily. A cloud of dust rose from the window ledge she was leaning against.

"Out!" Chiara shouted, "I'll be back later." Her mother exploded with a torrent of Italian profanities as she rode down the dusty street.

Sweat trickled down Chiara's forehead and the back of her neck. Her thick hair was soaked with it. She kept telling herself, "Tom will understand." She pedalled as fast as she could for more than fifteen minutes, pulling up alongside the mudflats to stretch her aching muscles. Ordinarily, she could cycle for hours but today at this pace her insides were screaming with pain. Her stomach knotted with spasmodic cramps and she could feel a dull throb in her head. The faster she cycled, the worse it became.

She stopped, dropped her bike under a mango tree and threw herself onto the grassy patch where she could always catch a sea breeze. Her head dropped, resting between her knees, her long hair spilling over to allow the breeze to cool her sweat-soaked nape and shoulders. Absentmindedly, she twisted her hair into a braid and knotted it on the top of her head like she had done a hundred times in the past, the curls keeping it in place.

Another cramp came on, causing her to huddle into a tighter knot until it diminished. "I need to talk to Tom," she thought out loud, "this pain can't be natural." Subconsciously, she decided that getting her period was the beginning of the end. The old Chiara, the girl with the insight of a wise old woman, was becoming a young woman.

It was very confusing. Maybe she won't visit Tom now? How could she discuss her period and the pains with him? He was her school friend but, as much as they talked about everything, maybe this was one secret she should keep?

She found herself thinking of Isabella and the gypsies. A sudden urge to join them overcame her and she wept as she realised it was never going to happen. Perhaps this was what the tower card meant? She often turned the tower card up in the secret tarot deck Isabella had given her all those years ago when she was a free-spirited Romany living on the streets of Rome.

Her thoughts turned to Tom as the cramp subsided. Sweet Tom had persisted until she accepted his friendship. He became the only living soul besides Isabella she could trust with her innermost secrets. Like her, he was reclusive and didn't like spending a lot of time with others. Tom had a way of understanding how she connected human life with nature.

She remembered his silly grin when she told him about her secret tarot deck that she always carried with her, and how he was fascinated when she read his cards. 'He always understands, after all, we are the same, me and him. His parents don't understand him either.'

She thought about how they met, and how he had always been there when all the others made fun of her. When she struggled with learning the new language, he patiently listened and helped her. Sometimes, it had taken hours for him to interpret a phrase or sentence in a way that she could understand. For the last two years, he had been her only friend and confidante. He knew her almost as intimately as she knew herself; he knew about Isabella and the gypsies and was fascinated by their lifestyle. He identified with her need for isolation.

Tom often sat patiently by her side while she talked about Italy and comforted her as she cried for home. He was the only one who had ever seen her tears, the only person she trusted, the only one she felt secure with and the only one she would ever allow to see the side of herself that was not the tough 'wog' kid which the other kids called her in the schoolyard. She was still a scared little girl who secretly wept for a life she was forced to leave behind.

After a while, she stood up, remembering the last time she sheltered under this very same tree. Tom was helping her with her English homework and she was struggling with pronunciation. As she looked at him, the sun was getting ready to set and the colours which danced upon the clouds were almost the same as the colours dancing in his hair. She saw him as a man, not just as a close friend. That was only three weeks ago, but it was a turning point in their friendship, a point where she must decide what their relationship was to be in the future.

She was so confused, everything was changing and she didn't like it. She wanted her life as it was, not the complicated mess it was becoming. She wanted her best friend to remain just that, she wanted to continue to be free, to be who she wanted to be and to keep her childlike innocence. Most of all, she wanted these agonizing cramps to go away, her body was changing faster than she could handle.

Neither the mango trees in the park nor the many shady Poinciana trees held any attraction for Chiara. She needed her confidante, her soulmate, and he was still quite a distance away. Seagulls scattered as she mounted the bike again and tentatively started pedalling as another cramp gripped her lower abdomen.

A film of dust was settling on her sweaty body, but still she kept a steady pace as she continued toward Tom's home. A train whistle blew in the distance as she approached the railway station. She decided to take a chance and cross the line as it was a shortcut to Tom's. He lived on the other side of the line.

Due to her throbbing head, she didn't realise how close the train was. If it hadn't been for the onset of another cramp, she would have cycled directly into the path of the oncoming train. She sat by the line, letting the bike drop to the ground, as she collected her thoughts, "This is crazy, I've never been this out of control. What is the matter with me?" she said aloud. After the train passed, she looked up and could make out the derelict house on the other side of the road.

Several laden coconut palms waved in the slight breeze. The front porch was disguised by a rambling philodendron that grew to the eaves. Chiara slowly straightened her body and pushed her bicycle to the front door. The house badly needed painting. As she knocked, clouds of dust swirled around her face causing her to cough.

She was struck by a stab of apprehension, "Maybe Tom won't understand," she thought. "How exactly does a fifteen-year-old girl describe her first period to a seventeen-year-old boy?"

She turned around and was about to escape when she heard heavy footsteps coming in her direction. "He thinks I'm as tough as one of those coconuts," she pondered as she looked at the laden tree and the renegade nuts that had found their way onto the verandah. She sucked in deeply as the footsteps rounded the verandah and Mrs. Flanagan came into view. She decided there and then that this would remain her personal 'girl' secret.

"Oh, it's you," her voice crackled in disgust. As usual, Mrs. Flanagan wore a filthy gingham apron over her grimy faded housedress which was in desperate need of mending. Her dirty orange blonde hair, which was usually in rollers, was today wrapped under a piece of old mosquito netting and stiff hairs like tiny orange needles stuck out through the holes.

"S'pose you'll be wantin' ma Tom, eh," she said with loathing in her voice. Chiara nodded in response; she saw no point in answering this woman as it always left the field open for sarcasm.

"Well, e's out the back, fixin' his bike," she said, as her beady eyes took in Chiara's expression. "Wassa matter, girl, ya not gunna go out back upsetting ma Tom, are ya?" she asked suspiciously.

"No," came the reply, thickly shrouded by her accent. As the older woman's eyes widened, Chiara began to panic inwardly, thinking, 'She knows,' as her feet began shuffling backwards down the stairs, her hands reaching out to the splintered rails for support. She was aghast that Tom's mother could tell what had happened to her.

She was sure it was so obvious when another cramp gripped her insides and caused her to buckle slightly as she fought to disguise her pain. "It is all right that maybe I go to the back and talk with Tom, please?" she asked, attempting to steer the focus from herself and the pain she was in.

"Eh," said Mrs. Flanagan who was always amused at the girl's accent. She broke into a malicious grin as she continued, "Ya wanna see Tom?" Chiara nodded in response, "S'pose, go on then, ya know the way," she snarled, spinning on her bare heels, and disappearing back around the corner. Chiara gripped the handrail momentarily as the pain subsided, stepped onto the verandah and entered the house.

Although she had seen it many times before, it astonished her that one family could live in such a jumbled mess of hoarded rubbish. There were endless piles of paper, toys, unopened boxes, chipped china, clean and discarded laundry, baskets of ironing which had found their way onto the floor and dirty, dusty furniture filling every square inch of wall space and a great deal of the window space as well.

The rooms were dank and musty and, because of the clutter, overwhelmingly dark as well. Even though outside it was still only mid-afternoon, inside there was an ominous gloom and an odour that was a mixture of mould from the humidity and lingering body odours from dirt, grime, and discarded belongings.

A playpen was pushed into the corner of the kitchen. Its grimy outline indicating that it had been on the floor for a long time. Baby Irene, who was now able to pull herself up and salivate on the grubby rails, had a pleading look in her washed-out eyes. Spent tears had left tracks on her pathetic little face and a saturated rag, which served as a nappy, barely clung to her tiny hips as urine dripped into a puddle around her bare feet.

The room was filled with nasty, pungent odours. The moisture had mixed with the dust on the floor and the resultant sludge had splashed onto the walls, the cupboard doors, the playpen rails, and her own little body, leaving grimy spots upon the multitude of stains on the walls, some of which had become mouldy over the years from the three other children who had occupied this spot in the corner of the kitchen.

Tom, now 17, was the oldest and his two brothers, Jimmy and Patrick were 15 and 12. And then along came twins, Duncan and Clancy who were now 4 years old and Irene who was the oops baby (and the only girl) conceived unexpectedly three years later. When her husband learned there was to be another child, he left to work on a sugarcane farm at Innisfail before she was born and never returned.

Many locals speculated that life with Mrs. Flanagan was so volatile that it was easier for him to leave, whilst others thought maybe something more dire had befallen him like a snakebite in the cane fields or a crocodile attack as he camped along the riverbank. These theories were feasible as he was known to be a heavy drinker and, even though he stayed with the other workers at the camp, he was prone to wander off in a drunken stupor from time to time which may have been why he was never sighted after he abandoned his family.

Regardless, Mary Flanagan was not coping well as a single mother of six children. Her mental health and ability to care for her younger children were deteriorating rapidly.

Chiara fought the impulse to turn up her nose at the child. Two years ago, when the playpen held a set of redheaded twins, the sight was nauseating to her, but she had seen it so many times since that she finally became accustomed to the squalor and the foul odours.

She was sure the blackened banana skin in the corner, which now exhibited a white fungus growth was the same one she had seen three weeks ago when she and Tom shared a cordial after that strange encounter in the park. She knew, as Tom did, that it was useless to attempt cleaning in a home of such misery where her efforts would not be noticed or appreciated.

Irene looked at her, her large sad eyes begging for any kind of attention, and she felt for the child as her tiny arms reached out to be comforted. Chiara gave her downy head a slight ruffle, and realised it was probably the most affectionate gesture the child had ever experienced. She decided against tackling the nappy as another cramping spasm began, and she grasped her stomach. This time the overpowering stench in the room brought on nausea and the persistent throb in her head exploded into an agonising pounding.

She covered her mouth and ran for the back door, knowing the outhouse was out there, and retched into the can which was filled to the brim with human waste and sawdust, the stench being even worse than it was inside. After the vomiting finished, she felt much better, and carefully sprinkled sawdust over the top of the can which threatened to overflow. She wiped her face and retied her hair which had fallen from the knot at her nape. Chiara turned to exit the outhouse and was mortified that in her haste she had left the door wide open.

In the small suburban backyard, a copper used for heating bathwater was nestled deep within the riotous growth and a children's swing set sat rusting and un-used. The overgrown garden was the result of years of neglect in the balmy northern tropics. It was a lush jungle paradise, if carefully nurtured, but an untamed wilderness when left to grow wild.

Through a tangle of rampant ferns and fallen palm fronds, she saw a familiar head of flame red hair bending over a tap as he splashed water onto the velvety ginger fuzz on his chest.

Hoping he had not witnessed her exhibition in the toilet, she found a way through the jungle of vines and ferns, stepping over a deep layer of discarded coconuts and mangoes, taking care not to become entangled in the spikes of the wait-a-while bushes that grew like weeds.

As she entered the clearing underneath the huge mango tree, scattered liberally with discarded skins and seeds, she heard Tom's mother yell from the kitchen. "Oy, turn the bleedin' water off, the tanks are almost empty as it is." From her vantage point, Chiara could see his eyes roll defiantly at his mother's crackling voice. He cupped his hands once more and splashed one final handful onto his face before snapping the metal handle of the tap. Instantly, the steady stream of water stopped,, the noise of which had stifled her approaching footsteps.

Still unaware of her presence, Tom stretched his body to his full six feet, his head and shoulders disappearing into the luxuriant curtain of leaves above.

Chiara watched in awe as the sun danced upon the golden down, highlighting the sprinkling of freckles upon his polished bronze chest. His long arms reached into the tree to pluck a ripe mango from a high branch. The tropical sun also caught the gold of his underarms and she wondered whether any other parts of his body were covered in the same golden fuzz. "This is Tom," she reproached herself, "I shouldn't be thinking about him in that way."

Lately, she had been thinking of him more and more, not as the friend he had always been, but as a young man, one she desired in a way she could not define. She didn't know what to make of her impulses. "What is going on in my head, why am I thinking like this all of the time, and why Tom?"

Her head was a riot of chaotic thoughts which were more troubling the more she tried to analyse them. She heard a rustling in the leaves. Looking up, she saw Tom's face, the boyish face she knew so well, looking back at her through the foliage and her bewilderment disappeared. His freckled face broke into a huge welcoming grin. Normality had returned, Tom was Tom, and she was simply his friend again.

"G'day," he said, "come and sit down over here." He pointed to an upturned pine box near where he was working on his bicycle. His hand reached up to pluck another mango and they sat together, sharing the juicy ripe fruit.

They didn't notice the scowling face at the window which grew darker when their hands touched as he passed her the mango. His mother never did approve of her kin associating with the migrants, but she was powerless to stop these two. They bonded from the very moment he laid eyes on her when she arrived as a bewildered thirteen-year-old who could not speak a scrap of English. To Tom, she was someone in need of his protection.

Chapter Eleven

Mary Flanagan was unhappy. Ever since the morning Reverend Jenkins introduced Chiara's family at church, three days after they had arrived in Cairns, she suspected Chiara of contaminating her son with her 'wog' ways. "Tom," she hissed, loud enough for him to hear, "I want ya to get me some wood for the fire and then fill up the copper and light it, eh, so the kids can 'ave a bath tonight."

Cheekily, Chiara knew it was a ploy to distance them so she answered for him, "That is a good idea no, I will help him, Mrs. Flanagan, then he will finish quickly and we can talk again more." Tom's eyes twinkled at her smart retort; he admired her ability to handle situations and not appear offended. It was an innate ability; he was amazed how she always managed to have the upper hand.

"Humph," came the reply. Mrs Flanagan could sense the friendship was developing into something stronger but to her chagrin, she realised it was out of her control.

These two were adolescents and whatever happened was fate, although to her mind it had the potential to become a fate worse than death. Through gritted teeth, she seethed, "I'll have to watch that Italian hussy with ma boy. I'll hafta talk to Gina at church on Sunday and warn her to keep that little harlot away from ma boy. That wild wog blood is nothin' but trouble and sure enough, that strumpet's gunna corrupt him."

As she clanked around the kitchen, cursing under her breath whilst making herself a cup of tea, she kept a watchful eye on the shenanigans outside. Irene screamed for attention and, as usual, she ignored her daughter's cries, continuing instead with her vicious tirade. "Bloody wogs, they never amount to nothing, be damned if one's gunna get her hooks into my son."

Out of frustration, she walked over to the playpen and slapped her baby daughter on her bare buttocks which were exposed because the wet nappy had finally fallen off. Irene shrieked as her mother slapped her on a red, inflamed rash, vowing as she did so that, "Hell will freeze over before those two ever get my approval. I'll never let a greasy wog contaminate our good Irish name, not even when I am taking my last breath on this earth."

The tirade ended as four-year-old Clancy came rushing in screaming, his twin brother Duncan on his heels. Duncan grabbed a lock of Clancy's hair and dragged him to the ground. Like a pair of wild animals, they fought desperately on the floor, their mother screeching for them to stop.

Finally, the bedlam stopped and both were dragged by their armpits to another room. They instinctively knew what was coming and they didn't have the courage to even whimper in protest, let alone resume where they left off.

The ominous silence, however, was soon broken by the sounds of a cracking whip which were followed by agonized howls from both children.

Whilst the insults bandied about the kitchen were barely audible outside, Chiara and Tom could clearly hear the children being beaten. Tom leapt up and ran inside to rescue them from further whipping by their sadistic mother. At 17, he was now big enough to stand up to her. He knew all too well what she was capable of, having borne the brunt of it for the best part of his life. He was not about to sit and listen while his brothers were abused and tortured the way he was.

It was this very violence that forced his father to drink to excess and finally to leave the family at the mercy of this woman they called mother. His father could no longer endure the daily physical and verbal torture from his wife. He promised Tom before he left that he would come back one day and take them away from this hellhole. But he never did. After the visits stopped long before Irene's birth, Tom gave up hope of ever seeing his father again.

Clancy and Duncan wailed pitifully as Tom took them into the backyard. He fetched a bottle of liniment he kept hidden in the laundry and applied it to their welts. Their young eyes pleaded for him to ease their suffering. He sat them on a log near the laundry and gave them a drink each from the tank and told them to be quiet for a while.

He knew his mother's rage would quickly settle and they would be safe from her again.

Her moods would swing from violent rage to quiet acceptance and during that time she would be an almost normal mother until again, without warning, she would snap and become enraged. She was completely unpredictable and life with her was a never-ending roller coaster of highs and lows.

Tom coped as best he could and attempted to shield the younger ones from her fits of rage. Most of the time, he was successful but they still suffered a great deal of physical and emotional scarring from her unpredictable violent abuse.

Chiara watched on, astonished that a boy of Tom's age was so mature. She admired the way he knew how to comfort his brothers. She could not comprehend how a mother was so monstrous as to beat her young children with such savagery.

Mary Flanagan was becoming more violent, more unhinged, and more dangerous as each day passed. Her paranoid thoughts about Chiara and her influence on Tom incensed and consumed her. She looked around at the disarray in the kitchen, at her filthy baby in the playpen, and finally at herself in the broken mirror hanging above the sink, and expressed her venom, "That bloody wog's caused this. We were a decent family before that tramp arrived."

She angrily grabbed the kettle simmering on the wood stove, "I got to figure out how to get that trollop away from my boy before she destroys us all." As she poured hot water onto a handful of tea leaves in a cup, she yelled out, "I'm goin' onto the verandah, don't none of you kids dare disturb me until I have finished, right!" There was no answer.

She stole one final look at Chiara and Tom who were deep in conversation by the laundry, her twin sons between them. When she saw his hand resting on Chiara's shoulder, she pulled a face and hissed disgustedly, "That bloody tramp's going to drag him in the muck and he is falling for it hook, line and sinker."

She turned on her heels and stormed out onto the verandah, obscenities flowing freely, and casually threw the china cup filled with scalding tea at the post on the verandah. She sat seething on the step surrounded by the shattered cup, mumbling incomprehensibly to nobody in particular.

Tom's room was a converted timber shed in the back corner of the yard. It was filled with old but clean furniture and was very tidy compared to the squalor of the house. He took a particular pride in keeping his own area clean and odour free.

Hanging from one of the beams was a kerosene lamp; an ancient wood stove was set into the very back of the room, the metal gleamed where Tom had meticulously scraped all the rust and debris from its surface.

Although cracked, the glass windows looked out on all four sides into the rambling garden littered with huge banana trees and passionfruit vines which threatened to invade the little dwelling. Tom kept them in check by trimming them regularly.

A wait-a-while tendril curled provocatively over the open doorway and the mango branches were low and obscured the entry so Chiara could not see the main house through the thick tangle of bushes and trees, even though it was only twenty feet or so away.

His mother, detesting the wait-a-whiles, never ventured this far into the yard so the little shed was his sanctuary, the one place Tom was free from her oppressive presence. It was dark inside the shed was dark due to the jungle around it and the palm fronds that dropped onto the roof. Chiara followed him into the room, leaving the door open as light was precious in this room.

Tom had a coconut in his hand from which he had deftly removed the husk with the spike in the corner, like his father had taught him many years ago. He inserted a screwdriver into the eyes at the top and offered Chiara a sip of the delicious clear fluid inside.

Chiara drank with relish; she was not overly fussed on the flesh of the coconut but found its clear liquid delicious.

"You don't look the same today," he said matter of factly, noticing that her olive but sun-bronzed skin had an unusual pallor.

"I'm alright," she said a little too quickly, causing his eyebrows to shoot up.

She wiped a trickle of coconut juice from her chin and looked at his face. Even in this semi-light she could see the brilliant emerald shine of his eyes as they searched her face for an answer as to what may be troubling her. 'That's the trouble with Tom,' she thought, 'he can read me too well.'

"You missed a bit," he said teasingly, reaching over and wiping a droplet of coconut juice from her chin and they laughed. His touch was electric and Chiara felt a jolt which she had never experienced before. Even though she was laughing, she averted her eyes and stared instead at a huge huntsman spider that was making its way across the floor. It lugged a massive white egg sac that was almost the size of the spider itself.

She concentrated on the spider to avoid conversation with Tom. "We should catch it so the twins see the little spiders when they hatch," she said absently rising at the same time to find something to capture it in. Tom had already risen and placed an empty jar over the creature before she had time to finish her sentence. It was amazing how often they both seemed to think the same thing at the same time. Again, she laughed.

He screwed the lid on and handed the jar to Chiara. She had never been frightened by spiders and this one was no exception. She found the creature fascinating and was absorbed in looking at it through the glass. She sensed that Tom was watching her which made her feel a little uncomfortable.

'The way he's looking at me is strange,' she thought when she finally met his gaze. "Will you play a song for me?" she asked, pointing to the old guitar in the corner of the room.

"If you want," he replied, feeling a little embarrassed about being caught staring at her. He had been marvelling at how beautiful she was becoming. 'I wish she would let her hair down; it is so nice and long and looks really pretty when she leaves it loose,' he thought, staring at her as she was watching the spider.

She took another drink from the coconut as Tom sat back on the bed and positioned the guitar.

Chiara lay back on the pillows as he began to pluck at the strings. The tune was horribly off key but it still sounded wonderful to Chiara. In a way, it reminded her of the gypsies and their endless music and dancing. For as long as he played, she was happy, lost in a nostalgic reverie.

Chapter Twelve

Ava was miserable. The miscarriage of her first baby turned out to be only the beginning. Every pregnancy ended the same way. A bloodied mess in the bed, on the toilet and once even in the hospital after the doctor ordered nine months of complete bed rest. She did not even make it to four months. At sixteen weeks, her body failed her again, and she fell into a despondent haze of melancholy.

With each miscarriage, Ava became less interested and her morose moods and depression became a fact of life. The doctors and nurses were unable to console her. The doctor informed Nico that, if the pregnancies and miscarriages were to continue, she would never be emotionally stable again. Depression had a firm grip upon her and, while each loss was heartbreaking, it became like the inevitable end which had become her life.

The doctor suggested to Nico that the best option might be to intervene surgically and prevent any more pregnancies. Ava would never agree and Nico feared their relationship would end if he spoke to her about it.

Under the pretence of looking under anaesthesia to try and fix the problem, Nico agreed to allow the doctors to remove her uterus. A hysterectomy she knew nothing about until half a year later when she realised she was no longer conceiving.

Robbed of ever being able to become a mother, Ava's frustrations turned to anger and hatred when she discovered that Nico had authorized the procedure. The person whom she trusted more than anyone had betrayed her. He knew how much she wanted a baby and she couldn't fathom why he took that chance away from her. She always felt that one of the pregnancies would be successful although, in the recesses of her mind, she feared it would probably not happen.

Nico agreed to the operation because he loved her enough to want what was best for her emotional wellbeing and most of all for the health of their relationship. This knowledge did not help her or make her feel better.

She was angry, bitter .... robbed. She was a woman, and a woman was meant to have children. How dare anyone take that God-given right away from her. She hated him for it, but deep within she also felt a sense of relief that the endless miscarriages were over.

Lost and unable to restore his grief-stricken wife to vitality and happiness, Nico penned a letter to her mother.

Outlining what had happened to his beautiful Ava, her daughter, he expressed his heartache at not being able to console her. As his tears dropped onto the paper, he sealed it and dropped it into the mailbox. He did not know what else to do. He was losing Ava and was grasping at whatever straws were left.

A letter arrived soon after. Her mother was bereft and wanted to visit but none of them had the funds to afford the journey to Australia and Nico was earning only enough money to pay for their meagre existence in Sydney. She included a letter for her daughter and in it was a suggestion that there was another way they could become parents. She said any child who was a part of their family, whether it was by blood or not, would be cherished by them as only a Nonna and Nonno could.

If they chose to adopt a child, it would still be a loved and cherished addition to their family. After reading this letter, Nico saw a glimmer of hope in the eyes of his wife. Her anger subsided but the despondency took time.

Adopting a baby had not occurred to them. The more she thought about it, the more Ava warmed to the idea.

The letters from her parents were now constant and Nico promised to put a small amount of money aside each week to assist with their passage to Australia in the future. This helped Ava to emerge slowly from her dark shell where she felt safe but so alone, and become the woman Nico fell in love with. It took time for Ava to recover her mental health.

She was far more cautious with her emotions and suspicious about her future but gradually she became happier and more contented with her life. Nico was so relieved. His beautiful Ava, the love of his life, the reason for his existence, was returning to him.

Eventually, they spoke with the doctor who performed the surgery and he agreed that adoption was a good option but there were several obstacles in their way. Life in Sydney was very expensive and they still lived in a boarding house which was not an acceptable home for an adopted child to be raised in. However, renting a house or even a flat in Sydney, especially without a car to travel in, was beyond the means of what he earned at the wharves.

No other jobs were available for a migrant worker in the area, regardless of how well he performed his current duties, or how good his references were. There were far too many people looking for employment in Sydney and the competition was fierce. So began the search.

Nico applied for jobs all over New South Wales, but none came to fruition. By chance, he saw an advertisement for a general labourer on a farm in Queensland and a home in the nearby town was included as a part of the employment agreement.

His application was accepted. Within three weeks, they were packed and on the train for the tiny township of Boggabilla which was close to the border of New South Wales and Queensland.

They were met there by Nico's new boss who drove them to the small country town of Goondiwindi, twenty minutes away on the other side of the border in Queensland and over three hours south west of Brisbane.

It was hot, it was dry and the ground was cracked, bare and dusty but Ava fell in love with the tiny weatherboard cottage on stilts with the huge wraparound verandah. It felt like home. It was a place to call their own. A place ready to welcome and raise their family in.

It was on the edge of the township but was in easy walking distance to the town centre. Arrangements were made for Nico to be picked up every morning by another worker. Once he obtained a driving licence, he would be provided with a car.

Life was finally starting to fall into place. All they needed was a child to complete the picture of their happy family which Ava had in her mind's eye. She was reassured the plan was evolving. The house inside and out badly needed painting and the roof leaked when it rained. The furniture was sparse and old and the wood stove billowed smoke from the chimney which left a smoke ring around the top of the high kitchen ceiling. But none of these defects were insurmountable problems.

She visualized her family on the verandah and saw her own toddlers playing on the tree swing and watching the kangaroos in the paddock below.

She planned where the vegetable garden would be planted and had chosen names for the chickens she wanted to put into the coop in the back yard.

"Yes, life here will be good," she mused. A gleam of excitement for the future appeared in her eyes that had been so sad and empty. They glittered, the western sunlight picking up their blue flecks. She felt alive once more.

The large rainwater tank was almost empty so they were told to be very careful with their water usage but even this information did not perturb her.

After living for almost three years in a room in a boarding house in Sydney, they now had a home and she had a dream, a vision for a life they could finally enjoy in a country that had only created bad memories and heartache.

Their possessions were few but before long she converted the sparse surroundings into a comfortable country cottage. Their home was charming and oozed a homeliness that she cleaned with pride. The townspeople accepted Nico and Ava with open arms and they were given surplus furnishings and useful items for the home. A curtain here, a rug there, tablecloths, tea-towels, even homemade tea-cosies, doilies and lots of pretty knick-knacks and utensils for the kitchen.

They were given a silky oak buffet in which Ava stored the pretty china pieces she was accumulating. It took pride of place in the small dining room and she polished it every morning until it gleamed.

The chimney was cleaned and the smoke ring was painted over. Saucepans served to catch drips of water from the roof when it rained and the house always smelt of beeswax and lemon. Living in their house was so different to the noisy traffic and the smoke and petrol fumes that filtered in from the bustling streets of Sydney.

In the country, the only sounds besides their happy chatter were birds chirping contentedly, squawking cockatoos and the pretty pink and grey galahs that congregated in the yard looking for grass seed heads and whatever else they could find. She especially loved the sounds of the laughing kookaburras in the trees close by. Ava waved to them from her verandah when she heard their song.

The scent of gum leaves after it rained became her favourite outdoor smell and she never tired of seeing the kangaroos as they hopped along by the back fence.

Often women from the town would drop by for a chat, to share a cup of tea and the special 'biscotti' she loved to bake. Spending time on the verandah with her friends whilst their children played in the yard below was a favourite pastime and baking biscotti was the other. Rural life suited her and she cherished the country people who were mostly friendly.

Ava was content with her country existence, and Nico showed his gratitude by often helping the townspeople with small jobs during his days off. They made many friends and gained the reputation of being a friendly and helpful couple.

Several weeks passed, and armed with a report from their doctor in Sydney which was a glowing recommendation that they be considered for adoption, they visited the local doctor who submitted the paperwork to the authorities. After all, he had a vested interest as well – his wife was very fond of Ava and wanted her to have the child she longed for. She saw how Ava was with her children and knew Ava would be an amazing mother. Together, she and her doctor husband penned another glowing recommendation which was actioned quickly.

Within weeks Ava and Nico were visited by a social worker, the home was approved, Nico was deemed financially secure and Nico's job was noted as long term with the boss stating that he was very happy with his new employee and their wives had also become close friends.

Convinced their marriage was stable and happy, the social worker believed they were perfect candidates for adoption, and from there the adoption process began. Ava was ecstatic. Her dreams were finally coming true.

She did experience some trepidation as she remembered the elation of her first pregnancy and the devastation of her loss. But she pushed her fears aside – this time her dreams of a family, however unconventional, were finally coming together. This time it was not her body that could fail her. For the first time in a very long time, she dared to hope again.

Chapter Thirteen

Chiara was settling into her new body. Soon to be seventeen, she was more versed in the ways of being a woman. Her closeness with Tom had become something more than friendship.

In the two years since Chiara's visit when she was fifteen, Tom realized how much Chiara meant to him. She was constantly on his mind. He would start to say something to her, forgetting she wasn't there. A cloud of disappointment would descend upon him. Was it love? He couldn't tell. Love had not been a part of his growing up which was about survival, one day at a time. A great many other changes had taken place in those two years. Tom's life was turned upside down.

Almost a year after their father disappeared, the three younger children had been removed from Mary Flanagan's care. Mary was ordered into an institution to treat her paranoid-schizophrenic disorder which had finally been diagnosed after yet another of her manic episodes.

The police came to the house one afternoon following a
report that Mary had pulled a knife on Tom when he tried
to intervene in a violent argument she was having with
a female church member about the state of her children
and home. The woman ran screaming from the house,
terrified that Tom had been badly hurt. Soon after, the
police arrived. Mary was taken away and admitted into
a care facility for assessment. The younger children were
placed into temporary care. The older three remained at
home and attempted to turn the house into a home.

That was almost a year ago now and Mary had progressed well. With medication and psychiatric supervision,
her severe mood swings were becoming less frequent, her
anger more manageable and the older boys were beginning
to feel like their house was a safe place again. For weeks,
they scrubbed, cleaned & cleared the home and yard for
their mother's imminent return.

Even though Mary was sometimes still a monster to
them and they harboured vivid memories of how she regularly abused them as they were growing up, they still loved
her and cared about her welfare. Her mental disorder and
lack of coping abilities to raise her six spirited children by
herself were the main reasons for her unpredictable violent
rages and the neglect and brutal beatings she inflicted on
her small children. Whilst it had always been in her, it
reached a peak when her husband vanished.

Jimmy and Patrick were excited but Tom was still unsure that his mother's return would be the happy home-
coming they hoped for. At nineteen, he was a man and had
left school several years ago to learn a trade, but the boy

in him felt he needed to be there with his family to shield and protect them. He could not forget the horrors of their past. He was still not convinced that life would be normal when she returned.

Irene was three now and the twins were almost 7 and they had settled in well with their new families. They were going to school and kindy and had made friends. Tom was worried about unsettling them from their newfound comfortable existence. Irene was so young when she left and only had vague memories of the trauma she had endured. He wanted her to stay where she was so she could continue to have a normal, happy life.

His only refuge during those years was the comforting presence of Chiara. Her frequent visits were like a shining beacon on a dark stormy night. She had a way of making the world feel not quite so heavy and him not quite so desolate.

One night, Tom was feeling overwhelmed by his responsibilities as the eldest son. That morning, he received the news that human remains had been found near where his father was last seen several years ago. He was waiting for confirmation they were the remains of his missing father.

'I don't know how I'm going to tell my brothers,' he was thinking when an even more potent challenge came into his head, 'How was he going to tell his violent, unpredictable mother?' A surge of emotion came over him. He slumped back on the bed and curled his body into a ball. Chiara reached out, her arms providing the solace he desperately needed. That embrace was the start of something they were not able to control. Their pent-up feelings for each other flared up.

Chiara lay down beside Tom, put her arms around him and nuzzled the back of his neck. Tom turned to face her. They kissed and clung together. Both as stunned as each other over the events they seemingly had no control over. They wanted to be closer, to have the touch of skin against skin. Peeling off their clothes, they lay together on the bed.

Unrestrained, they explored each other's bodies. Tom was filled with wonder at her beauty. Tenderly, he touched her and tasted her sweetness as he explored her naked body. Chiara's hand stole shyly down his body, amazed at the strength and hardness of his masculinity. She felt hypnotised and instinctively she guided him towards her.

It did hurt and, when she cried out, he pulled back and continued to kiss and stroke her until she became more aroused. Several minutes later, he murmured, "Is it ok – can I?"

She gasped, "Yes, oh yes."

The second time Chiara knew what to expect and, when she felt the stinging pain, she urged him to keep going.

From that night on, they became inseparable. When they were in each other's arms, no one else mattered, nothing else existed except for what was happening in that small room at the back of the garden and the two people comforting each other in sweet, tender, sexual bliss.

Chiara knew she was playing a dangerous game and eventually it caught up with her. Several months after her seventeenth birthday, she noticed changes in her body and her feelings. Her breasts became larger, harder, and painfully tender and her mood became blissfully calm. It was as if she didn't have a care or a worry in the world. She realised that her monthly bleeding had stopped and in a panic she worked out that she had already missed four periods. Her midriff was getting larger and she felt tiny fluttering movements in her abdomen.

She knew what all these signs meant, but she went into a state of denial. She refused to think about it or how she was going to deal with it. She didn't say anything to Tom although she had started to do so on a number of occasions but somehow, she couldn't get the words out. He would have to know about the baby, that he was going to be a father in about five months.

But his mother was returning soon, his father's memorial was being organised and his dysfunctional family life were all bearing down on Tom. She didn't want to add to his mountain of burdens. So she decided to keep away from Tom before he could notice she was pregnant. After all, solitude and isolation was no stranger to her.

She had never really spoken with her parents about anything personal. She was scared about how they would react so she kept the secret from them too. Maybe if she ignored it, it would go away which she knew was ridiculous. It was never going to go away but she was not ready to face up to telling her staunchly Catholic parents that their unwed and underage daughter was having a baby.

Chiara was already into the third trimester, and it was becoming difficult to disguise her bulging midriff.

Tom had taken his mother to Townsville for a few months to reacquaint her with the younger children. The authorities would only allow visits if she was accompanied by Tom who was now a legal guardian of his mother's affairs. Consequently, he did not see Chiara at all from her fourth month onwards.

Things came to a head when a visiting church woman spoke with her mother about her suspicions. Together, they spoke to Chiara, establishing that she was indeed expecting a baby and it was only 12 weeks away from arriving. She did not need to divulge the father. They all knew how close she and Tom were and there was no doubt he was the father. Her mother was most unhappy and felt humiliated that her daughter would be so wanton and irresponsible.

Mary Flanagan was not well liked in the town. The people considered her children were too wild and free-spirited to ever become responsible citizens, let alone be capable of raising responsible children.

Of course, Chiara knew how responsible Tom was and how he would make a wonderful father. But it would be useless to try and change their opinions about the Flanagans. Gina knew she needed a plan, and fast, to be able to hide this indiscretion from the prying eyes of the people of Cairns.

Once her parents knew about the baby, matters were rapidly taken out of Chiara's control. Her parents decided she could not stay in Cairns and bring shame to the family. With the help of the church, she would be sent to Brisbane to a home for unmarried mothers. Within a few days, she was on a train heading south with a chaperone from the church to accompany her and ensure her safe arrival.

The Matron greeted them at the door, took her details and her luggage and the chaperone was sent home. The doors were locked behind her and Chiara was alone in Brisbane with a baby growing inside her. Tom was still in Townsville until next week and was totally unaware of her situation. She had no way of contacting him. She had been cast out of her home, she was alone and scared, completely abandoned by her mother and father whom she thought loved her.

She looked at her single bed in the dormitory and surveyed the other girls who were in varying stages of pregnancy. She felt suddenly overwhelmed by the gravity of her situation. In under three months, she would be a mother. How was she going to provide for a child on her own? As she was still 17, the law stated that her parents had sole control of the baby's destiny.

Unbeknownst to her, they had already agreed and signed the paperwork for the baby to be placed up for adoption immediately after birth. As a minor, Chiara would have no choice but to agree.

During the next 12 weeks, Chiara worked in the hostel laundry and shared meals in the hostel dining room. Her pregnancy was uneventful and she made friends with the other girls but no outside interactions or excursions were allowed. It was a kind of a prison. They were allowed an occasional walk in the hostel's gardens which were kept safe from prying eyes by a high brick wall and a large wrought iron gate which was secured by a heavy chain and padlock.

One by one, the girls gave birth. Chiara came to understand that most of the babies born there were adopted out after birth. Initially, she thought the girls were relinquishing them voluntarily but then she realised that most of them were her age and they had no choice. Keeping their baby was not an option.

Only one girl was able to keep her baby when her 23-year-old boyfriend arrived before the birth and they were married. Becoming husband and wife prior to the birth enabled them to be able to keep the baby in their care.

Chiara tried to send letters to Tom but they came back with 'Return to Sender' scrawled over them. His mother was intercepting her letters which appeared to have been opened and resealed before being returned, so she was almost certain Mary was aware of her condition.

Her parents didn't come to see her at the hostel. She neither received any mail from them enquiring about her health, or how she felt about the impending birth, nor did she write to them. The parent-child relationship was fractured and Chiara's attitude was bittersweet.

For once in her life, she needed her mother by her side, but her streetwise arrogance would not allow her to admit it. She missed her father dreadfully. He was always the calming influence in her life. She wished she could sit down and talk with them about what was happening and how she was feeling.

Gina and Enzo never spoke with anyone about their daughter's situation and nobody asked why Chiara was away. It was generally assumed that she went to Brisbane to do a course. No one questioned her absence as it was acceptable for a girl to leave home at seventeen to study.

In the same week Chiara was due to give birth, Mary Flanagan had another episode that resulted in an injury to her back. She was admitted to Cairns Base Hospital, however it was ill equipped to deal with her physical injuries coupled with yet another mental breakdown.

Tom, still unaware of Chiara's pregnancy, watched as his mother was sent to a Brisbane hospital that could treat her for both conditions. Mary Flanagan was back for an extended stay in the same institution which had previously housed her.

Chiara penned what was to be the last letter to Tom before the baby arrived. As she placed it in the hostel mailbox and began to walk back to her bed, she felt a gush of water and stood still as a large puddle accumulated around her feet.

The nurses swiftly arrived and confirmed Chiara had gone into labour. As she was taken into the birthing room, she felt the first pangs of her baby's imminent arrival.

Chapter Fourteen

Several days later, Tom and his brothers were home alone once more. Their younger siblings were sent back to the families that had previously cared for them. Tom collected the mail that afternoon. Seeing his name on the envelope in a familiar handwriting with an unfamiliar address on the back, he scratched his head. The letter read:

'Dear Tom,' I do not know if any of my previous letters reached you so I do not know if you are still unaware of my situation.

I am sitting here on my bed in Brisbane in the home that has become my prison, waiting to meet our child.

He or she should be here within the next few days. I have been told I will have no choice but to allow the baby to be given to another family. This is the law and unless I am married or my parents have agreed to care for it, I cannot legally keep it as I am still considered to be underage.

I have said that my wish is that the child be placed with another Italian family but I know this may not happen. All I hope is that our baby has a good life with a good family. If you get this letter and can be in Brisbane before the birth, I am in the Catholic home for unmarried mothers in Ashgrove, a suburb in Brisbane. It is run by the Church and they are very strict about visitors, men especially, however the address is on the back of envelope, hopefully you can find it and be here in time.

I probably will not return to Cairns afterwards. I think my parents are ashamed and life with them will no longer be pleasant or free and I am certain they will not allow me to see you anymore, our friendship can never be the same now. They have never spoken with me since they sent me here. The Matron told me my parents have organized a boarding house for me to move into. I do not know the address there but I can tell you that I have been enrolled at the Secretarial School in Kangaroo Point in Brisbane for the next term which starts in January next year.

I have a few months to recover and decide what I would like to do. The Secretarial School is not far from here and I think maybe learning is a good idea. I could become a good secretary and marry a nice man and have many more babies. Who knows what the future will bring but one thing I do know is that I will always remember you and the child we made together.

Your friend forever, Chiara."

Tom was dumbfounded. He stared at the letter in a state of shock and disbelief. What other letters was she talking about? Chiara had left abruptly without even telling him she was leaving. He hadn't known what to think. It was not like Chiara to go without any explanation. Her parents had fobbed him off, shaking their heads, saying only that she was with friends in Brisbane. This was the first letter he had ever received from her.

It was as if a bolt of lightning had come from a clear blue sky and struck him. He couldn't move and he couldn't think straight. He was about to become a father. A glass wall had shattered over him and he was sitting amongst the shards, not sure how to deal with the mess without getting hurt. He was angry that Chiara's pregnancy had been kept from him all this time.

Why hadn't Chiara told him?

Why did her parents not mention it? Did his mother know?

So many questions, but first he needed to see Chiara.

The next train was leaving in three days and it took almost three days to get to Brisbane. Even then he needed to get to the hostel to see her. Would he make it in time?

Would they let him see her?

Would he be able to see the baby after it was born?

He did not know – with everything he had, he was going to try.

Chapter Fifteen

It was early October 1960, four years since they arrived in Australia. Their naturalization had proceeded without a problem, and they were now Australian citizens. Everything was in place except for one unavoidable detail.

In one month, Nico would be thirty-five; the age limit for adopting was 35. By November, it would be too late.

Hope was fading fast and Ava was beginning to feel that familiar pain of loss as she saw her dreams disappear as the months flew by. Luckily, she had her home and her many friends whom she cherished. They kept her from slipping into that dark place that engulfed her after she suffered the miscarriages and was denied her life's ambition to become a mother.

They had been in Goondiwindi for a year now. As usual, Nico had left for the day and Ava had finished sweeping and polishing her prized buffet.

The aroma of freshly baked biscotti cooling on the windowsill wafted out onto the verandah as she looked down the dusty dirt road for her friend Judith to arrive for their morning chat over tea and biscotti.

Only this time, it was different. Judith was running, not walking, leaving a trail of dust in her wake as she came down the dirt road in the heat with a heavy toddler in her arms.

Her young son demanded to be put down so he could practise his walking, but she was not going to be slowed down. Not this time.

Today Judith had to get to Ava quickly and was out of breath by the time she reached the gate.

Ava was worried. After all, Judith was the local doctor's wife and she thought maybe something had happened to Nico or there was an emergency. All kinds of scenarios flashed through her mind, each one worse than the last. She ran down to meet Judith at the gate.

Out of breath and sweating, Judith managed to say, "You had a phone call, the agency .... the agency is ringing back in 20 minutes .... You need to come back with us .... Now."

Ava had no idea what the phone call meant but she relieved Judith of the heavy toddler in her arms. Together they ran back to the surgery, kicking up dust and puffing in the heat the whole way.

With only enough time to get their breath back, the phone rang and Judith answered, passing it to Ava immediately.

"Mrs. Palladino"

"Yes – this is Ava Palladino."

"Mrs. Palladino, a child has just been born in Brisbane. The mother has asked if it can be placed with an Italian family and you and your husband are on the short-list. We need you both here 2 p.m. Friday afternoon for a pre-screen and interview." Ava let out an audible gasp; her hand flew to her mouth and her eyes widened. She could not believe what she was hearing.

"You have a baby for us?"

"Yes Mrs. Palladino. If you are successful after the interview, you will have a baby girl to take home with you on Friday."

Ava was speechless, she could not manage anything more than a shaky "thank you" as she fell into the leather chair behind the doctor's desk. As happy tears began to fall, emotion took over. Speech was no longer possible so the phone was passed back to Judith.

"I am sorry, Mrs. Palladino is a bit overcome at present. I am Doctor Jackson's wife. Can I take all the details of where they need to be and we will ensure they will be there?"

Judith began hastily writing notes on a pad in front of her, names and telephone numbers were exchanged and what they needed to bring with them was listed.

Judith hung up the phone and the women embraced, Ava dissolving into tears, not quite believing what was unfolding. Three weeks was all they had left. Three weeks and Nico would be 35. Three weeks and their dream would be over. This was their last chance.

A baby girl, she could not believe it. It did not feel real. After she collected herself, she looked at the list. "We have none of these things," she said – we have not prepared for a baby as we did not think it would happen so fast."

"It's OK, Ava, you can have all our son's things until you can get your own, we have a bassinette to bring her home in, and my husband will drop the cot and baby bath and anything else you will need to your home while you are away."

At that moment Ava knew she had a true friend as Judith continued "You can have all of Joey's baby clothes, and we have baby milk formula and bottles in the clinic cupboard. You can take those with you." All you need to buy are nappies and we can do that after you and I drive out to tell Nico the good news."

Ava's shoulders shuddered and she began sobbing and Judith held her close until it subsided. Judith held her hand as they walked to the police station.

It was a country town, after all, and the young constable did not hesitate when Judith said it was urgent that they go to the farm immediately. Ava needed to speak to Nico and it could not wait until tonight. It was already Tuesday and the interview was Friday.

Nico was given the rest of the rest of the week off so they could prepare everything for the baby. The time moved at warp speed. There was so much they needed to organize and there was nowhere near enough time.

By this time, Nico was an experienced driver so his boss lent him a car for the trip to Brisbane. The bassinette from Judith was placed on the back seat in the car. Judith gave them several sets of the tiniest clothes Ava had ever seen. A soft pale blue bunny rug that was used for Joey went into the bag to bring the baby home in.

The bag went into the car together with the bassinette, a dozen nappies with pins, bottles, a saucepan to boil water and sterilize the bottles and a large tin of baby formula. Nico kept asking Judith if they needed anything else. He was sure they had forgotten things, but Judith assured them they were well prepared.

Receiving many hugs and best wishes for a safe journey, Nico and Ava said goodbye to their friends and left early Thursday morning.

It was a long, arduous trip with some difficult road conditions due to recent rains. Nico drove slowly through the slippery mud. Coming through the mountain pass, the road ahead was winding and shrouded in mist.

Many places on their journey were bumpy and filled with corrugations and other areas were smooth bitumen. They talked about their little baby girl, about driving her home on such a bumpy road and were filled with excitement about what awaited them in Brisbane.

It was almost dark when they arrived. They found a hotel that had accommodation above it, close to the hostel where they were having the interview the next day.

Ava remembered the hotel in Fremantle and clung tightly to Nico as they asked at the packed bar for a room.

She need not have worried as the men at the bar were not at all interested in them and carried on with their drinking and conversation, unaware of the couple going up the stairs.

It was a clean, bare room, containing a bed, a cupboard and a door that opened to the large verandah overlooking the busy road below. The bathroom was at the end of the hallway and the toilet was an outhouse downstairs. It reminded them of the boarding house in Sydney.

After bathing, they prepared for bed. Before they retired, they opened the large map of Brisbane which could easily cover a tabletop and studied it for the trip tomorrow. They knew the address wasn't far from where they were staying but, as they had not been to Brisbane before, they worried about getting lost. The map was checked, and checked again, and then Nico used a pencil to mark the roads to follow so that Ava could direct him.

They tossed and turned all night, finally drifting into a light slumber in the early hours. Even though the appointment was at 2 p.m., they were dressed and ready to leave by 9 a.m. They did not know how long or how much traffic they would encounter, whether they may get a flat tyre or any of the other scenarios that played out in their minds.

A quick breakfast in the café opposite the hotel and by 10 a.m. they were on their way, arriving without incident at noon. It was two hours before their interview was due to happen.

The building was a huge brick fortress with a large wrought iron gate at the front and a bell to ring to get attention.

When they were finally let in, they were met by a stern, sturdy woman wearing a starched nurse's cap and a pristine uniform.

Her black leather shoes gleamed with polish and she bowed politely as she ushered them to a set of benches in a small waiting area outside an office. It was 12.30 p.m. Another couple were seated in the waiting room.

Ava tried not to be obvious but couldn't help staring at the woman who, looking very prim and proper, sat stiffly beside her husband. Her sleek blonde hair was tied into a tight bun at the back of her head. She exuded an aura of superiority. Was she looking down her nose at them, a migrant couple with no city presence about them.

She probably thought they were uncivilised country folk and, if they were the competition for the child on offer, there was no contest at all. The woman sat with her legs crossed under an expensive-looking tweed skirt, she glanced at her well-dressed husband who was busily reading a newspaper, then looked back at Ava and Nico. There was an air of arrogance about the way the woman scanned them from head to foot.

It was obvious that she was from a wealthier part of town. The husband was relaxed and projected self-assurance. He was younger than Nico and she was older than Ava. An austere and proper Australian couple with a status and a lifestyle Nico and Ava could not possibly match. Ava became increasingly nervous and fidgety. Will they be successful today?

The other couple would have everything to provide for a new baby and they had the class and finances to raise a very well educated and successful child. All Ava and Nico had to offer was a comfortable home and a loving family in a small country town. They had many friends there but no extended family – will that be enough? The other couple were ushered into the office. After about ten minutes, the couple exited again.

Ava clutched Nico's arm as she watched them walk proudly out the door. Ava didn't know if that was what was meant to happen. Did they get an answer straight away, or did they have to go home and wait to be notified? Were the other couple successful and would they return for the baby later. Ava was beside herself with nervous tension.

Through the doors opposite the office, another couple Ava had not seen before exited with a baby.

"Is that her, is that the baby we were hoping for?" she thought, as tears began welling in her eyes.

She heard the couple talking with excitement in their voices, "He is perfect, his name will be Michael. I can't wait to get him home."

'Thank goodness,' Ava said silently, 'Their baby is a boy, our baby girl is still there, we still have a chance.'

Finally, they were brought through into the office. Nico remained calm but Ava was shaking with anticipation and nerves. Her legs turned to jelly as she sat opposite the Matron who introduced herself and opened a file on her desk.

The stern matronly face broke into a flicker of a smile as she revealed they were the last interview and the only Italian family to be short-listed. As it turned out, what they thought would be an interview turned out to be the pre-liminary signing of documents which the Matron passed to them one after another.

"Congratulations, Mr. and Mrs. Palladino, you now have a twelve-day-old baby daughter." It was the moment that changed everything. Ava dissolved into a pool of emotion while Nico smiled and nodded as he tried to maintain his composure. From the other side of her polished oak desk, the Matron beamed at them, and said, "Her birth mother named her Isabella and requested that the baby be brought up with Italian values and culture. You may change the baby's name as soon as the adoption is registered. A new birth certificate listing you as parents will arrive in a few weeks. Do you have any questions?"

In the car trip to Brisbane, Ava and Nico discussed naming her Sophia after her mother and grandmother but they had not yet decided on a middle name. There were no family members who Nico wished to honour and Sophia (the first and second) had no middle names so they now had a decision to make. The adoption papers would be lodged by the Matron and the new name would appear on her birth certificate.

There was time; all they wanted right now was to take their daughter home.

"Would you like to meet her?"

Ava nodded so hard she feared her neck might break. They followed the matron through the same door that they saw the couple exit from with their new son Michael.

They were taken to the nursery to meet the baby and do a final check to ensure they were happy with the health and state of the baby, but they had already decided she was theirs.

There was no question in their minds. Even if she had two heads and three legs, they were not leaving without her. And together they walked to the waiting nurse who showed them the baby, stripped naked and stretching her legs and arms as if waiting to be held.

Ava looks at baby Isabella as she wriggles in the nursery basket. She is perfect. Dark chocolate eyes, a very light olive skin and a crop of dark ginger hair as if sunlight had been sprinkled on her tiny head. She recalled the young girl on the boat all those years ago and how fondly she spoke about her gypsy friend named Isabella and for some reason it felt right. So it was decided at that moment that Isabella was the name she would have forever. It would not be changed.

The only difference would be the addition of her mother's and her Nonna's name as a middle name to honour the two most wonderful women in her life. She looked at Nico and said "I have a name, is it alright if I choose?"

"Of course," said Nico in his soothing, gentle voice. Ava turned to the baby and said, "Hello, Isabella Sophia Palladino, would you like to come home with us?"

Surprised by his own strong emotions, Nico hugged his wife and kissed his new daughter on the forehead as the nurse placed her in his wife's arms. Ever so gently, he embraced them both and they cradled the fragile infant as a family.

Overcome with joy, Ava gently handed her to the nurse for changing into the clothes they brought with them. She watched in wonder as she squirmed and wriggled whilst the nurse dressed her.

Nico did not realise how much of an impact such a tiny baby would have on him but, from the moment he looked into her dark eyes and her red fuzzy hair, he was bonded to her forever. With Ava by his side, their little family would be a blissfully happy one.

Ava handed over the blue bunny rug to wrap Isabella snugly for her journey to the hotel. As she did so, the nurse revealed a small document she had secreted under the baby's back. Ava furrowed her brow and the nurse whispered, "It's her original birth certificate." She made a shushing motion with her lips and flicks a furtive glance around the room before continuing, "One day, she will ask who her mother is. This document contains all the details she needs, if you decide to tell her. But you must never tell anyone where it came from or who gave it to you."

Ava and Nico glanced at each other. They understood the nurse had broken all the rules of adoption, but were grateful she had the foresight to provide them with this valuable link to their daughter's heritage. They nodded and pretended they hadn't seen anything.

With Isabella awake but blissfully content and securely wrapped in her bunny rug, the nurse placed their baby in the bassinette that Judith gave them. But Ava cannot help herself. She reached down and picked her up, breathing in her newborn daughter's heady scent.

Holding her tightly, they left with their new daughter in her mother's arms and the name of her birth mother on the document hidden in Isabella's bunny rug. Driving at a pace that could almost equal walking, they returned to the hotel for the night. They sterilized Isabella's bottles in the hotel kitchen, adding the powder for the evening feed and two bottles for overnight.

Isabella was sleeping contentedly in the bassinette but Ava and Nico were on tenterhooks all night long. They checked on her constantly, making sure she was there, that she was safe and breathing well. Isabella was fed and changed shortly after midnight and again in the early morning before they left on the long trip back home. Their baby daughter was tucked up and sleeping in the bassinette on the back seat.

The trip home took many hours longer than they anticipated. They stopped often to change Isabella's nappy and to prepare a bottle which had to be warmed. They stopped at every town and asked shop owners to warm the bottles. Before leaving Brisbane, they filled the sterile bottles with boiled water and sealed them. All that was needed was to add the powdered formula.

It was late evening when they drove into their house yard. The trip took 11 hours and they were exhausted. Isabella hardly made a whimper during the entire time. They felt so blessed as they carried their sleeping daughter upstairs to what would become her home.

Chapter Sixteen

Tom was beside himself. Panic was setting in. He needed to be with Chiara. He needed to be a father to his child. He needed a family of his own away from all the madness he had experienced in his life. He was in love and wanted to be with Chiara, but he was terrified.

Everything he loved in this world was ripped away from him or resulted in unimaginable pain. His mother, his father, his siblings, and even Chiara left without a word. Nothing ever ended well. He was scared: scared to trust, scared to love, scared to hope. No matter where he went in the world, his demons followed. Chiara was the closest he ever felt to being alive, feeling, hoping, loving. But then she was gone. Nothing. Emptiness.

But a baby? A baby was innocent. A baby was new life, new hope. If only he could get there in time.

Her letter was dated 10 days ago, on the 6th. Tom read it repeatedly, sitting on the train for Brisbane.

The world passed by outside at a snail's pace. He needed it to go faster. He sighed heavily; he desperately needed to be there. His frustrations ate away at him as he banged his head softly against the carriage window. His tousled red hair fell over his taut face and clenched jaw.

Sunlight highlighted the ginger fuzz on his biceps, every muscle twitching as he willed the train to move faster. Sleep was elusive, short naps that ended in frightening dreams about the chaos surrounding him.

People were looking at him. Some of them had expressions of disapproval on their faces. He had not shaved in a week; his hair was mess of red tangles and his clothes were dirty and ragged. He did not care that he looked like a hobo. He needed to be with Chiara. All he could think of was embracing Chiara and their child and leaving the madness behind, once and for all. There was no plan – only an urgency. A race against time to do what needed to be done.

He woke with a start, "The train will be arriving at Roma Street in 15 minutes," the voice on the PA announced. After the long train journey, it was now 13 days since the letter had been written and Tom was frantic.

"Finally," he thought. "Now I need to find where this place is."

He looked in his wallet, there was not much in it, ten pounds and a few shillings. Enough maybe for a taxi and to pay for a train back for himself, Chiara and the baby but certainly not enough for accommodation.

"OK, first things first." He grabbed his dirty duffel bag and made his way to the door. When the train stopped, he banged on the glass until it opened and he ran. He did not stop running until he was on the street. Cars everywhere, buildings and, as luck would have it, a taxi was by the kerb. Sliding in the front seat, he barked the address to the driver and told him to drive as fast as possible. The taxi wound through streets, dodged pedestrians, and Tom felt it was going even slower than the train.

"Geez mate, can't you go a bit faster?" he pleaded, but the driver ignored him and kept weaving and winding through brick high-rises, the wide muddy brown river by his side, huge bridges, and timber buildings on stilts. Many were surrounded by stately gardens and an endless stream of picket fences. He had forgotten how big Brisbane was.

Finally, Tom arrived at a large ominous-looking iron gate. He paid the cab driver and rang the bell repeatedly. Nobody came, he yelled to the front door and finally a stocky woman in a nurse's uniform came out and met him at the gate.

"I'm here to see Chiara Calvecchio," he said frantically.

"We cannot allow that. No girl here is allowed visitors."

"You do not understand, she is having a baby, my baby. I need to see her."

"I'm sorry Mr. ......?"

"Flanagan, my name's Tom Flanagan, I need to see Chiara." Tom rattled the gate but the chains and padlock held it securely. He looked pleadingly at the nurse. "Please, it's important, I got a letter from her. I didn't know about the baby; I need to see her."

"That's not possible, Mr. Flanagan."

"Why?" he asked, raising his voice slightly.

"Because the girls here do not have visitors unless they are family."

"I am family!" he screeched. "The baby is mine" ...... "our baby is due to be born, I can help her, I want her to keep it, I want us to keep it." Chiara!" he yelled, "Chiara! I'm here. Chiara! We can do this, I will marry you, we can keep the baby."

"Mr. Flanagan, you need to calm down. We cannot help you, it's too late," she said, with a deadpan expression on her face.

Reality hit Tom like a bolt of lightning. Frantically searching for answers, he raised his voice louder, "Is it already born? When, when – I need to know. How are they? Where is Chiara?"

In desperation, Tom shouted his demands at her and bashing against the gate with his body.

The nurse stepped back. She was appalled by his raging anger and threatening tone. This dirty, dishevelled man was making demands. How dare he come here! The child was fortunate to have gone to another home. There was no way this hobo would know how to be a father.

She gave him one more indignant glare, turned around and strode off, leaving Tom yelling at her from the gate.

"Please, I need to see Chiara, let me see Chiara," but his frenzied pleas fell on deaf ears. The heavy timber and wrought iron door slammed shut and he was again alone. But Tom was not giving up. He pulled the bell and rattled the gate until the rope on the bell broke, after which he started yelling.

After almost an hour, another woman came out. This one was much sterner looking than the last.

"I want to see Chiara; I won't leave until I see her."

"Mr Flanagan," she said abruptly. "This is a hospital. We have people here who need rest, you must stop."

Tom persisted and kept on shaking the gate, causing the chains to strain and rattle. He was becoming incoherent as he grew more anxious and afraid.

"If you don't stop, we will be forced to call the police."

"Just let me see Chiara, then I'll leave."

"Miss Calvecchio is no longer here. You must leave immediately."

"Where is she, is she OK? What about the baby?"

"Mr. Flanagan, she has left and so has the baby. It went to a new family yesterday, and Miss Calvecchio is no longer with us."

"Where is she?" he demanded

"I cannot tell you. Arrangements have been made and she is recuperating. That is all we are at liberty to tell you." Tom was aghast, his hands slid down the iron gate, and he dropped his head forward, muttering incoherently.

"Neither Miss Calvecchio nor her child are here so you see it is pointless to continue with this charade. Please leave the premises now before we call the authorities." With that command, she spun on her heels and marched to the door.

Tom turned and slumped against the gate. He had never felt so defeated in his life. 'Where could she be? The baby was gone. What can I do?'

Realising there was nothing left to do, he stood and limped away, defeated. It was early afternoon and Tom walked. One foot in front of the other. Not looking, just walking. He had no idea where to; he walked aimlessly like a lost soul. As the sun started to dip over the horizon, he realised he had no idea where he was. Looking around to get his bearings, he felt even more lost. At this point, he did not care. Life was meaningless, pointless. Everything was gone.

Seeing a park in the distance, he started towards it. Sitting on a bench, he attempted to get his thoughts together but they were scattered and he could not think of a way to fix the situation he was in. How could he find Chiara? He was not going to give up.

Looking at the letter again, he thought maybe the Secretarial School but that would be useless; she was not starting there until January. Kangaroo Point, she said she was staying in a boarding house near the Secretarial School. "That's it, I'll go to Kangaroo Point and look there," he mused wearily.

Exhaustion was taking hold; the heat and the hours of walking made him weary. It was getting dark. His mind was shutting down. Sleep was now his friend and his eyelids were heavy. As he put his head on his duffel bag, right there on the park bench his eyes closed, and he succumbed to sweet slumber. Occasional dreams penetrated but he slept soundly until he was woken by a jolt. Something or someone was poking him in the ribs.

"You can't sleep here, mate," said the police officer standing over him. "You need to go."

Tom blinked. He was still half asleep and didn't recognise or remember his surroundings. "Where am I?" he said, confused, "What time is it?"

"It's 5 a.m. You're in Spring hill. This park is not a good place for you to sleep, mate, it can get dangerous here"

Still in a sleep-induced fog, Tom rubbed his eyes and everything flooded back. He was in Brisbane, not his room in Cairns. Chiara had the baby and they have both gone. He's lost everything he ever cared about. Now he was wide awake.

"Sorry, I just came from Cairns. I didn't mean to fall asleep here, I had a big day and wanted to sit and think for a while. How do I get to Kangaroo Point?"

The officer pointed to the river. "It is not far, head for the river and cross the Story Bridge. It's right there. About an hour's walk away."

Tom stood up, stretched, and wiped his eyes. He shuddered as his body began to wake up.

The policeman warned, "Just watch yourself. This area can get bad."

"Thanks," said Tom and he shook the officer's hand. He turned to grab his bag and noticed his wallet had fallen to the ground. Fearing the worst, he checked and his cash was still there but for safekeeping he tucked a 5-pound note into his sock.

"Good idea," said the officer "Now, get moving before I charge you with vagrancy." Tom set off towards the river. As he was walking across the bridge, he looked at the buildings on the opposite side.

There were so many houses, 'Where will I even start? Maybe I should follow the river?' he mused. He followed it to a huge bend and right in front of him was a large shipyard. Before he had time to think it through, Tom approached a foreman on the wharf and asked him about work. He thinks that, maybe if he has a job in the area, he will be able to find where Chiara is living. Who knows, one day he might see her walking down the street. It's a long shot but he has run out of ideas.

As luck would have it, they were short a worker that morning and so his job began, building ships on the river at Kangaroo Point.

That evening he checked into a hotel close by and had a bath, a hot meal at the bar and a proper bed to sleep in. The ginger mop is still wild and knotted and he desperately needs a shave but he is feeling like, maybe, he might have a way forward.

If he has a job, finds Chiara, they get their baby back, maybe everything will fall into place.

Over the next few days, his skills with a hammer and nails do not go unnoticed and soon he is offered an apprenticeship as a builder. A shipbuilder, but a builder, nonetheless. Surely shipbuilders can also build houses, he thinks. This was what he wanted to do, build homes and maybe one day, he would build his own home for his own family. This trade would hold him in good employment for the rest of his life.

His future was looking better, now all he needed was Chiara.

Chapter Seventeen

Mentally and physically drained from the long car ride to bring their new daughter to her forever home, Ava and Nico pulled into their driveway. They looked at the house and then the sleeping infant in the back of the car and, in a moment of reflection, they understood. After the turbulent events leading up to this moment, and the feeling that it may never eventuate, they stared at each other and silently acknowledged that everything was finally right in the world.

For all its ups and downs, turning their back on the Palladino family's power and money, marrying against their wishes and migrating to Australia was the best decision they had ever made. A surge of calmness enveloped them.

At just thirteen days old, baby Isabella, with her angelic features, had made their eventful and often traumatic journey worth it.

Nico lifted the basket, careful not to disturb her, and deposited it on the verandah at the top of the stairs. Whispering he will be back shortly, he hurried down to help Ava with the luggage and baby items they purchased in Brisbane.

Ava noticed the baby was waking and squinting in the last rays of sunlight. She lifted her gently out of the basket. Together, they stand at the top of the stairs, the sunset catching the glints of gold in their hair and sparkling like a thousand fireflies.

Nico paused at the bottom of the stairs, the sight of his wife and infant daughter in the golden light was sublime. For a few seconds, he was lost in a reverie, thinking, 'Life at this moment could not be better.' As they stood at the threshold of their new life as a family, the fading light framing his wife and daughter was the most wonderful vision of their glorious future.

Shaking himself out of his dreamy musings, he brought the last item up the stairs. Together, the family walked into the small room at the back of their home which would be Isabella's bedroom.

Astonished, they stood in the doorway in total awe of the scene in front of them.

Whilst they were away, the townspeople had come to-gether and transformed the room into a pretty nursery that would be fit for a princess.

Gone were the bare timber walls devoid of any decora-tions. Now they were painted the palest pink, made more beautiful by the streaks of pink and purple reflecting from the sunset on the western horizon.

White linen curtains with tiny pink and lavender but-terflies adorned the bare windows and an exquisite silky oak wardrobe took pride of place, standing at an angle in the corner opposite the door. Gleaming and polished to a shining brilliance to match the buffet in the dining room, the full-length mirror reflected the astonishment of the couple standing in the doorway, their baby daughter in her mother's arms.

A changing table with the softest padded fabric was next to the handmade timber cot placed underneath the eastern facing window. Complete with a mattress, side protectors and pale pink sheets, it was made up and ready for Isabella. Opposite the window, an oversized armchair was covered in the most adorable hand-knitted baby blanket Ava had ever seen.

Stepping into the room, Ava opened the wardrobe which was filled with baby girl's clothing. Even a crocheted bonnet with a matching jacket and booties were folded on the change table. A huge rug had been placed on the floor to soften their footsteps on the creaking wooden floorboards.

They slowly turned and gazed in wonderment at the framed pictures of fairies, butterflies and gumnuts adorning the walls. Under the framed pictures, they saw a large pram and a small camphor chest filled with assorted soft toys.

Nico selected a small brown bear and placed it in the cot. "For you, my Bella, already the world is in love with you."

And so it began, Bella, the most beloved word in the Italian language for beautiful, became the name by which the world knew Isabella Sophia Palladino.

Caring for an infant was daunting. They had a steady stream of visitors. All were taken by the beauty of tiny Bella and, as she grew, she became more and more mesmerizing. Her dark eyes seemed to reflect a deep soul, almost as if she had been on the Earth before and had seen much.

The ginger fuzz grew into copper curls and each day they became redder and more intense. When the sunlight hit them directly, the curls glowed with a life of their own. Like dancing copper flames, they swayed in the breeze.

Nico & Ava were in love with their child. Nothing was ever going to be too much for her. Bella was thriving.

Several weeks later, Ava was sitting in the armchair feeding Bella, Nico watched on in amazement at how perfect the scene was. Outside, the sun was high in the midday sky and a mob of kangaroos bounded past the fence line. Sunlight streamed in the window, reflecting off Ava's lovely blonde tresses, highlighting the soft serenity of her features and dancing like a golden halo on his daughter's flaming copper curls.

There have been so many moments since they brought their daughter home when he has said, "Life could not be any more perfect," but then another moment was created. Each memory surpassed the last and they were all etched forever in his mind.

In the armchair, Ava sat and admired the sleeping infant or cradled her in her waking hours, thinking how blessed she was to have her own child who will now and forever call her mother. She had a daughter, she had a husband and a home, and together they were a family.

The first Christmas brought wonderment as they shared it with Judith, her husband, and their children. The Christmas tree was plain, a gum tree branch secured in a bucket of sand but lovingly decorated with shiny garlands and strings of tinsel and so many baubles. Bella stared at the sparkling angel on top and the many prettily-wrapped presents scattered around the base.

A wooden train and tracks for Joey with a handmade station and tiny people he could move along the platform, a dollhouse for Angela complete with tiny furniture and miniature dolls that she could dress and place in any of the pretty rooms, and for Bella, a lovely doll with long red hair and eyes that opened and closed.

"The doll's name is Faye," said Judith, "That was the name on the box, feel free to change it if you wish."

"No, Faye is the name she was given and Faye it will be," Nico assured her, "Bella will love her new companion, thank you very much."

Christmas dinner was delicious, very different to an Italian Christmas and even to the Christmases they had in Sydney. This one was their first as a family and the first with a family and it was special because of the immense amount of love and genuine friendship that flowed between them all.

The next day was a holiday and Nico and Ava enjoyed his day at home with their almost three-month-old daughter. They propped her up among a pile of pillows on the verandah as they all enjoyed a cool summer morning breeze.

As always, the parents were close by, Ava sat on the floor, her arms circling the child in case she fell forward. Nico was on the chair opposite, watching her every expression and movement which had become his favourite pastime.

Bella gurgled contentedly at all the colours and shapes around her. She was captivated by a beautiful red and black butterfly that settled on Ava's shoulder. They watched in amazement as their daughter laughed for the first time, her little arms reaching clumsily towards it. The butterfly fanned its wings and was unperturbed.

Nico commented how Bella was such a fitting name. "She is our beautiful butterfly, our Bella butterfly."

They agreed her name was perfect for a child as beautiful as a butterfly; Bella butterfly, radiant, exquisite and with an air of heavenly magnificence.

Chapter Eighteen

Chiara was sleeping. Her body was recovering from the birth twelve days ago. She jerked awake, looking from side to side, her eyes wide. Everything came back to her in a rush.

'What happened to my baby?' was her first thought. 'I felt it, I heard it cry. Why did they hold up a sheet so I couldn't see her?' She had so many questions running through her mind. She felt so empty. It was baffling. She had been sucked into a giant void and could not find a way out.

"The nurse told me it was a girl, and said she was healthy. Surely seeing her would not be so bad," Chiara muttered to no one in particular. "Maybe I could sneak into the nursery and take a peek." She lifted herself slowly off the hard dormitory mattress.

One quick glance around the room revealed no one in sight. 'I can do this,' she told herself. Treading softly, she made her way through the door and along the hallway to the room beyond the birthing quarters. She was close. There was a door at the end of the hallway.

Still nobody around, she cautiously opened the door and grimaced as it creaked. No one was in sight and she could hear a baby softly crying.

Slowly she stepped into the room, it was empty except for one wriggling infant in a bassinette.

The baby could smell her milk and screamed to fill its little tummy.

But it was not her baby. It was an Aboriginal baby.

Where was her baby?

Where was Isabella?

The screams brought a nurse hurrying in. She was startled to see Chiara scanning the other bassinettes. "You can't be in here," she whispered, "The girls are not allowed."

"I wanted to see my baby" she said. "Where is she?"

The nurse looked at her with soft gentle eyes and said in a quiet soothing voice, "You have to go back to your room, I can't help you."

"Please tell me," she pleaded, "Is she OK, where is she?"

"Yes, she is fine, go back before the matron catches you. All hell will break loose if she sees you here."

"Please just tell me."

Footsteps were coming down the hall from the front end. "You need to go now."

"Tell me, please."

"Your baby was adopted earlier today, she is gone."

"Adopted, were they nice?"

"Yes, very nice, now please go. If the matron catches you here, I will lose my job." The footsteps were getting closer and the nurse began to panic, pushing Chiara towards the back door.

"I need to get a message to her father. His name is Tom Flanagan."

"OK," she said as she pushed Chiara out the door, "go now, I'll see you later this afternoon when the doctor comes for your check-up."

Chiara closed the door just before the matron entered through the front. The nurse breathed a sigh of relief and the baby in the nursery stopped crying

Later that afternoon, the nurse accompanied the doctor on his rounds. Chiara slipped her a note with Tom's name and address on it.

Matron made her appearance, stating in her no-nonsense way, "Well, Dr Morgan has given you a clean bill of health, it's time for you to move to the boarding house. Your parents are happy for you to be there as early as next week if you are feeling up to it."

"Are my parents coming?" Chiara asked, not expecting they would be.

"No, dear, but they have left some money with the boarding house supervisor and your room is paid until next year when you can start your studies. It is time to move on with your life."

Chiara was defeated. She had lost the will to fight and accepted her fate. The law said that at twenty-one she could do as she pleased but she was not yet even 18. A year at a secretarial school seemed like hell. She could not see herself sitting in front of a typewriter for the rest of her life but for now she would do as she was told. Her rebellious spirit had been temporarily tamed.

She put her head back down on the hard pillow and curled her body into the foetal position. She squeezed her eyes closed. She wanted to live her life her way. As she drifted off to sleep, her thoughts were of Tom and their baby girl and what might have been. She awoke minutes later to a commotion outside. Somebody was yelling, it was a male voice and it was loud and angry. But it was too far away to make out what he was saying.

The door burst open and a nurse hurried in. Chiara looked at her perplexed, and the nurse told her to remain on her bed and insisted she had to stay in her room.

The window was pulled closed and the curtains drawn. When the door was closed, the noise outside became muffled and barely audible but strangely the nurse stayed in the room with her.

Eventually, the noise subsided and the matron came in. She whispered something to the nurse and they left the room together. Chiara heard the key turn in the lock. "That's strange, why have I been locked in?" She rushed to the window but it did not face the area where the yelling was coming from, so she sat on the bed and waited.

She wondered whether the matron found out that she had been in the nursery and this was why she was locked in. She hoped the nurse didn't get into trouble. Did she still have Tom's details or had she been caught?

'Never mind, I'll write him a letter and send that tomorrow.'

Finally, after several hours her door was unlocked. It was dark outside now as the matron stood by her bed and said in a solemn voice, "There has been a change of plan. You will be leaving in the morning. The boarding house has a bed ready for you and they are expecting you. Make sure you have all your possessions packed by tonight as the transport will be here shortly after sunrise."

Chiara blinked and her brow furrowed. 'What's going on? Why are they moving me so suddenly?'

The housemistress at the new hostel was very strict and listed the many rules as she showed Chiara her bed in the room she will be sharing with one other girl. The rules were many; no boys, no smoking, no swearing, no loud music. No leaving without permission, and only between 9 a.m. and 3.30 p.m., and only if prior approval was sought & granted.

There was a roster in the kitchen and everyone has chores. The bathtub and sink must be cleaned after use. No water to be left on the floor, no makeup, no nail polish, and towels must be hung up to dry, not left on the floor. Clothes must be clean and presentable at all times and no revealing necklines or short skirts.

Rooms must be kept tidy and beds must be made every morning with bedding changed every Saturday. The housemistress stated that she must always know where the girls are, and so on. The list was endless. Chiara felt like she had simply left one prison cell for another.

Thankfully, one saving grace was Carole who gave her a quick wink and a smile when they were introduced. At least hers was one friendly face. They will be at the Secretarial School together in January although Carole mentioned that, if she was able to find work, she may not go to Secretarial School. Carole seemed to be a little less stiff than the other girls in the common room. 'Maybe life in Brisbane will not be so bad, after all?' Chiara hoped.

Time moved on, Chiara and Carole shared a lot of laughs and played cards after lights out. She talked fondly of her home in Chinchilla and how her father was the local police officer there. She admitted to Chiara that she doesn't want to be a secretary but it was her way of being able to leave home. She really wanted to explore life in Brisbane but it was not going to be easy with the 'prison warder,' also known as the housemistress, watching their every move.

Gradually, Chiara settled into life there and before long it was mid-November. Just over a month until Christmas and the girls were getting restless.

The housemistress agreed to let them go to the city for the day and do some shopping.

The city was busy and exciting as they hopped on one tram after another which took them to opposite side of the river and back again. They went for a leisurely stroll through the Botanic Gardens, watched the ferry as it took passengers to the opposite shore and marvelled at the statues in the city square.

They giggled and laughed like schoolgirls all day long as they explored the streets in the Valley. David Jones was beyond anything either girl had ever seen before. The happy tunes of the man playing jazz pieces on his piano made them twirl and dance and laugh, and dance some more.

Heavily made-up shop assistants stood at the perfume counter with endless bottles which they sprayed on the women who walked past. The girls had an amazing time experimenting with nail polish until every finger was a different colour. Chiara sat and allowed a beautician to paint her face. She loved the sky blue eyeshadow and ruby red lipstick and how the foundation made her olive complexion look so smooth and pale.

She barely recognized herself as she looked in the mirror. She certainly did not look seventeen. She could easily pass for much older and Carole looked adorable with her pink blush and Marilyn Monroe pout.

"The housemistress would have a fit if she saw us now," Carole laughed as she grabbed Chiara's hand and pulled her towards the fashion section. The bright full skirts with flowers and fitted tops, white knee-high boots, brightly coloured dresses, vibrant stripes, and midriff tops in every colour of the rainbow. The girls were in heaven.

In the city, they bought a few small token trinkets as Christmas gifts, some cards and wrapping paper. Finally, they bade goodbye to the fashions and the fun. Reluctantly, it came time to make their way back across the Story Bridge. On the tram, they wiped the make-up off their faces, memories of the day still vivid in their minds.

This day of freedom was what Chiara had been longing for. She knew she was not meant to be a secretary. She did not speak to Carole about her plans, but started to plot her escape from that day on.

Chapter Nineteen

It was now February 1961 and Tom had been in Brisbane for four months. Every day of the week was the same routine.

Wake at sunrise, bathe, shave, enjoy a coffee and fried bread with bacon before grabbing his sandwiches from the hotel kitchen and walking out the door.

Most days, even early mornings, the sun was fierce so the sunglasses and Akubra he found by the cliffs provided a welcome relief on his morning walk.

Strolling past the Secretarial School he stopped, as he always did, near the entrance and scanned the horde of students arriving for the morning classes. He was searching for any sign of Chiara, but she was never among them.

After the morning surge settled, he continued past the cliffs, along the winding street, and down the steep decline to the bend in the river.

He worked hard all morning until the whistle blew for lunch. It was always the same ritual. Grabbing his sand-

wiches and hat, he walked up the hill to the Secretarial
School and repeated the morning's scrutiny of the people
going in and out the front door. Several people watched
him suspiciously. But he didn't seem to pose a threat. He
ate his lunch, waiting for the girls to go back in, and headed
back down the hill to finish his afternoon's work.

By 2 p.m., it is too late. Most of the students have
already left for the day so he took the trip home along the
river at the base of the cliffs and past the park. Perhaps she
might be there with her friends or having an afternoon
stroll.

Finally, back at the hotel, he repeated his evening
regime. A wash, change out of his sweaty work clothes,
reads the newspaper until about 7.30, then headed downstairs for a beer and a meal. Tonight, its pork sausages, peas,
and mash. Bidding the publican goodnight, he retired for
the evening.

It was a quiet existence; for the most part it suited him.
The room was plain but clean with his bed and a basin and
a few clothes in his duffel bag, but he didn't want to clutter
his surroundings. He clung to the hope that someday he
will see Chiara again, and will take her back to Cairns
where they can start their life together. So he made sure he
only had what he could carry with him.

On Saturdays, he enjoyed a sleep in, and rose at 8 a.m.
to catch the tram to the city, followed by a leisurely bus trip
to the outer suburbs near Ipswich.

His mother had been in Goodna for four months now
and every visit he noticed small improvements in her condition.

She was always pleased to hear the news from home and especially about baby Irene. Although Tom knew little about his sister, he spoke to his mother about how Irene's birthday was approaching, and how she might have a party at kindy with all her friends. He knew any conversation about Irene kept her happy and her mood level most of the time

He brought a letter from Jimmy who moved to Townsville a few months ago. Jimmy wrote that Irene was now with a family in Proserpine. The home was large with many other children and she was thriving. She looked happy and well when he visited last and the foster mother was a really good cook. She would often serve Irene's favourite fish fingers with hot chips and tomato sauce.

"Her hair is getting long now," he wrote, "she looks so pretty with her pigtails and red ribbons." Tom stopped before reading out the next sentence, 'Don't tell Mum this, Tom, but Irene told me she wants to stay there forever.'

His brow creased as he thought what to say. "School next year," he added, catching that familiar twinkle in her eyes. "Soon there will be six candles on her birthday cake."

"Jimmy said he'll try to get a photo but no promises, OK."

"OK." Mary was satisfied. She closed her eyes and thought of happy times ahead. She would try harder this time. Her children were being cared for and, in her mind's eye, it was only a matter of time before she would see them again. It gave her hope.

He unfolded the letter from Patrick who was still in Cairns.

'Tell Mum we had a cyclone further up north and the wind was really bad here.'

Mary became slightly agitated and her eyes widened. Tom recognised the signs. He needed to ensure she had no reason to become anxious.

"Luckily, there was not much damage to the house, Mum," he said. "It stripped all the coconuts and mangoes from the trees, and my room in the shed at the back got a beating, but the house is fine."

He didn't mention the roof damage or that Patrick had assured him it would be fixed before Mary was released from hospital.

"Tell Mum the twins are doing OK as well. They go to church every Sunday with Mr & Mrs Wallace and are getting ready for grade five next year."

"The Wallaces love having them. They even took them camping after they went to visit Jimmy & Irene these holidays. He signed off with, "give Mum a hug from me and tell her we all love her and hope she gets better soon."

"Ahhhh," she sighed. "You are good boys. Your father would be proud."

She closed her eyes and smiled contentedly.

Tom was silent as he studied her face. The medical reports said her back was getting better, her mind was improving and she wanted to go home.

But Tom was not so sure. He was worried but what could he say? It was up to the doctors.

Eighteen-year-old Jimmy was four hours away on a trawler near Townsville and Patrick, although he looked and acted like a grown man, was still barely 16.

Patrick still lived in the house and the twins visited regularly when he was not away working with the cane cutters. Tom knew about Patrick's plan to move away after their mother came home and had settled in. He was talking about heading south to spend time with Jimmy or the other possibility was to work on a farm further inland or on the Tablelands. He hadn't made up his mind yet.

Tom needed to stay in Brisbane. He too was uncertain of his future. Although he had a job, he was still secretly hopeful that he could find Chiara and the baby. When that happened, he would work out where they would go to start life together as a family.

Mary was happy to hear the boys were settling into a life of their own.

She was keen to start afresh with the twins and Irene.

In her mind, she had painted a picture of a perfect family. Her pretty little doll she could dress up and show off to the world and her well-behaved older sons who would take care of them all. This was her sanctuary and she believed with all her heart that this was how it was going to be when she returned.

Tom had reservations. The younger ones were finally settled in their new homes. He was concerned his mother was not ready to cope with three spirited youngsters on her own. But he could not be there anymore. That part of his life was over. He was resigned to that fact. His mother was in the hands of the doctors and God, and he prayed they would keep a close eye on her and keep the youngsters safe.

Tom could only be there as the dutiful son and wait for it to implode again as he was certain it would.

The one time he mentioned Chiara during the first hospital visit all those months ago, she lapsed into a simmering rage.

She began yelling expletives about how the girl had destroyed his life and brought shame on the family name.

She hissed incoherently, "The secret, it's a secret and we don't tell secrets."

She recovered quickly from her chaotic ramblings which to the outside world was a short insignificant episode, but he knew.

In her mostly lucid times, she didn't divulge what she had learned from Chiara's letters, the ones she never passed on. Tom never mentioned that he had received a final letter and already knew the secret she was trying to keep from him.

He never told her that Chiara was the reason he was in Brisbane in the first place. It was easier to let his mother go on believing he was there for her.

They never spoke about the baby, although it was apparent she knew, and that she was the one who concealed it from him for all those months leading up to the birth.

She was the reason he had lost his chance with Chiara, lost his chance with the baby, and he could not forgive her for any of it.

He never spoke her name again. He sat there quietly, every Saturday afternoon, the ever-compliant eldest son, doing his duty, watching, as she switched from happy to angry, her face changing from a scowling, furrowed brow and gritted teeth to sparkling, happy eyes in an instant. It was like watching a mime artist change from a taut, angry face to a beaming smile within seconds.

Sometimes, she was bewildered for a second, confused, then instantly she would be ecstatically happy again. He knew no other normal, this was life with his mother and, like the dutiful eldest son, he made sure she was safe and content. He would share a Saturday afternoon lunch with her, kiss her on the cheek and leave her to her deluded thoughts about her future which was going to be perfect.

Luckily, the doctors agreed with Tom, and Mary was kept at the facility much longer than expected.

As time went by, Tom slowly came to the realization that Chiara may never again be a part of his life and that he would never meet the child they created together.

He eventually stopped going to the cliffs every day, sometimes choosing to eat on the docks instead, listening to the chatter around him. He was only going through the motions of life and nothing much changed around him. The calmness and repetition was a soothing respite from the previous chaos of his life in Cairns which had brought him to this new normal calmer existence in the bustling inner-city centre of Brisbane.

He still visited his mother every Saturday and was slowly adjusting to this new world. A world without bedlam, a world without fear of the unknown. He began to see a future for himself.

Maybe he was ready for a change, he mused. But he remained unsure of what that change would be.

Then one day he stopped looking. He didn't peer anymore into every shop, or wait at the doors of the Secretarial

School, or walk past the seats at the front scrutinizing every group of girls just in case.

And finally; he stopped remembering.

He forgot the fresh smell of her auburn hair as she rested her head on his shoulder. He forgot the comforting warmth of her embrace when his world was crashing down around him. He forgot how secure he felt exposing the deep dark parts of his soul to her.

Most of all, he stopped wondering where their baby might be.

A whole year later, Mary was finally cleared to return to Cairns. She was happy at the prospect of being reunited with her precious daughter and accepted that the twins had decided to stay with their foster family for another year.

Tom felt that life for his family may finally become semi-normal.

1962 was almost over. He stood on the train platform, saying goodbye to his mother. He was surprised by the warm embrace she gave him before she stepped on to the train for home. Unaccustomed and slightly immune to any affection from her, he was taken aback.

He saw tears in her eyes and a gentleness in her face that he hadn't seen for a long, long time. The memories of a little boy sitting on his mother's lap overwhelmed him, and he turned away before she saw his tears. He was a complicated soul and yearned for the one who understood him because, God knew, he couldn't understand himself.

He walked away, wiping the evidence of his sorrow from his cheeks. A beautiful black & red butterfly danced in front of him. It occurred to him that his life, like that of the butterfly, was short.

The dancing butterfly was like a beacon, lightening his spirit and softly leading him towards his future life. Instinctively, he let the butterfly lead the way; after it left him, a new calmness washed over him. He knew what he must do.

Chapter Twenty

It was three months since Chiara's baby was born. Lately, she had been thinking less about Isabella and more about becoming free to live a life of her own choosing.

Peering under her bed at the plain brown leather suitcase which contained all her worldly possessions, Chiara began to activate her escape plan.

The suitcase had been her constant companion since childhood. Chiara felt a nostalgic twinge as she recalled how huge it seemed when they were hiding in the cellar. Her father had to carry it for her when they boarded the boat, then to the dilapidated shack in Cairns. When she was sent away, with her belly showing, she had to carry it and it was large.

But in this boarding house in Brisbane, her old suitcase was nowhere near big enough. There were things she must keep secret if she is to slip out unnoticed.

Tomorrow will be the first day at Secretarial School; she needed to do this now.

She checked – yes, the clothes from David Jones, how she loved the jeans with the huge flare and flowers on the pockets and the miniskirt that the housemistress would confiscate if she was caught wearing it.

Make up, lipstick, eyeshadow, foundation, even a tiny mirror. Yes, it was all there. The money she had been saving from her allowance was in a brown paper bag secreted under her clothing.

Everyone was sleeping. "Well, it's now or never," she said under her breath.

She quietly slipped down the hallway, past the housemistress's door and stops. A final check. Complete silence except for the creaking floorboards beneath her bare feet.

Using the cover of the early morning darkness, she made a dash for the thick bushes near the park at the end of the street.

She crouched down, checking for any sounds or movements. Nobody was around, "I need to be quick," she said as she slid the suitcase inside the large rosemary hedge, double checking that it was completely secreted in the dense aromatic shrubbery.

To remember its exact position, she made a mental note of the large flowering flame tree in the park behind her. She pushed a small stick into the ground, topping it with one of her small, red hair ribbons. She stepped back to take note of the surroundings.

"Good, not even a hint, that should be right till morning."

Satisfied her secret was safe and only she knew a suitcase was concealed there, she took the short journey back to the boarding house, rounding the corner and breathing a deep sigh of relief when she saw the house remained in total darkness.

She cautiously padded barefoot up the front steps and slowly opened the creaking door on the verandah. Stopping, she let out an audible gasp, "Oh my God, Carole is awake."

Panic set in as she searched for an excuse as to why she was outside in the middle of the night.

"Where have you been?" Carole said sleepily, "You know if you're caught out after lights out, there'll be hell to pay."

"It's OK, I went for a walk. It's so hot inside tonight." She added, "Is the Warden up?"

Carole giggled at their pet name for the housemistress, and shook her head. She was satisfied. Soon after Chiara arrived at the boarding house, she discovered she was her own person. There was a free spirit inside her that would never be fully tamed. Chiara will always do what Chiara chose to do.

Chiara checked in the large tallboy at the foot of her bed that her clothes and handbag were ready for tomorrow. She breathed a sigh of relief as she climbed back into bed. Closing her eyes, she tried to go back to sleep. But sleep was elusive. Thoughts of the day to come flickered through her mind, like moths around a candle flame, and doubts crept in about whether she was doing the right thing.

Her doubts faded as she remembered why she made the plan to escape. Secretarial School was a world away from her dreams about her future. Her gypsy heart and soul could not be stilled, The best days of her life were when she was with the gypsies in her homeland. It was where she felt happy and settled.

She closed her eyes and imagined what her future life would be. Who could say where this journey would take her, but for now, she must sleep, tomorrow would be a big day. The start of a new life. A life she was choosing to live.

Tossing and turning, drifting in and out of restless slumber, Chiara finally welcomed the first slivers of sunlight streaming through the window.

She was nervous, excited, and bursting with anticipation of what the day would bring. But she had to remember to act as she normally did, especially now.

A quick clean up in the bathroom, a change into the clothes prepared the night before for her first day at Secretarial School; only this time she stuffed her pyjamas into her handbag, along with her toothbrush, toothpaste, a comb and a bar of soap.

Like every other day, she went downstairs for breakfast. A final sweep of her room after eating. Good, nothing was forgotten.

"Well, Chiara, today will be the first day of the rest of your life. Are you excited?" the housemistress enquired, her arms folded across her chest.

"More than you would ever believe," she said truthfully, thinking that a more honest statement could not be spoken.

She bade the housemistress goodbye, hugged Carole, wished her the best at her new job and headed toward the park.

Chiara located the case easily. Nobody was around. Good, she continued walking past the intersection that would have taken her to the Secretarial School . She went towards the closest tram stop and, after a short trip, found herself standing in the middle of West End, a place she had been warned never to go, because it was dangerous and filled with lowlifes and criminals.

West End was not like they described it. In fact, it was quite the opposite. She loved it! So many Greeks and Italians and immigrants from the Middle East called this place home. Shops were filled with their wares and delicacies from their homelands were everywhere.

The streets were lively and noisy with people speaking many languages. Some she recognised, others were foreign, but they appeared happy and contented to be living within this small world of many cultures in Brisbane.

Chiara was drawn to these streets which felt to her like a refuge for people who didn't fit in elsewhere. "Yes, I will fit in here nicely," she murmured, as she carried her suitcase into a public restroom. With a quick change of clothing, a pair of platform shoes that boosted her height by an extra two inches and a bright red scarf tied around her head to hide her black curls, she morphed from a young lady not quite 18 to a woman at least 5 years older with a swagger and a confidence which only someone with a world of experience could carry off.

Wearing her snug-fitting midriff top, flared jeans with the embroidered flowers on the pockets, blue painted eyes, and ruby red lips, she walked into the closest hotel.

"Good morning," she said confidently. "I've just arrived from Sydney and I was wondering if you have any work available?"

"What have you done?"

"I can cook, clean, serve meals and I am a very quick learner."

"Have you worked behind a bar before?"

"No, but if you show me what to do, I'm sure I will learn."

"Can you start today?"

"Yes." she replied, surprised how quickly he offered her a job. Not once did he even question her age. She was shocked at how easy it was.

"Where are you staying?" he asked.

"I was hoping to find somewhere today?" she blurted out, telling herself, "Slow down, be confident."

"There is a room upstairs if you want it, what's your name?"

"Chiara, Chiara DeRoma" she said, without flinching at the tiny name change.

"OK, Chiara DeRoma," he said without a hint of suspicion, "take your case up to room 9, you turn left at the top of the stairs A night-time meal, lunch and breakfast will be provided and pay day is every Friday. Be down here by three o'clock and you can start in the kitchen."

" Chiara could not believe her luck. Inwardly she was ecstatic but outwardly she kept herself in check even though she wanted to do a happy dance as she carried her case up the stairs.

For the next three weeks, she peeled and mashed potatoes, washed pots and pans, cleaned, and served meals, learned how to pour a beer without ending up with a huge head of foam and many of the other jobs in a hotel.

She heard that several weeks after she arrived, the police came to the hotel whilst she was working in the kitchen. They had Chiara's description and explained that her family was looking for her, but the owner kept her presence secret. He didn't know what she was running from and he didn't care.

She was a good worker, the Italians loved her, and he didn't want to lose her. She could speak their language and the stories she told, especially about the streets and the gypsies, made everyone nostalgic and homesick. Yes, she loved her new life and her new life loved her.

Weeks turned into months, months turned into half a year and by then she was a part of the West End culture. She loved the Turkish bakery and the Lebanese takeaway. The thrift shop had become her second home. Room 9 at the top of the stairs was filling up fast.

She was gaining quite a collection of bohemian clothing and scarves which she tied bandana style over her bouncing curls in an attempt to keep her identity secret.

One cool winter afternoon, whilst chatting with a few hippies enjoying the sunlight at the back, she heard of a room in a house not far from the hotel. Seven others lived there and they all shared the kitchen and the bathroom. The closed-in verandah was available and the rent was very cheap. That afternoon, she told the hotel manager she was moving out. By Saturday, she was snug and warm in her huge verandah bedroom.

Sheets and surplus scarves from the thrift store became curtains over the louvred windows, crocheted blankets became her bedding. A chest of drawers and a mirrored duchess from her Turkish friends became her first real pieces of furniture. She promptly painted both of them bright orange with a glossy black trim and covered them with tiny painted flowers and butterflies.

As she curled up in her own room, under her own sheets, with her own furniture, she realised that she was finally free.

The bar owner never mentioned the police again, and when she saw them on the streets, they didn't even look her way. Her new clothes, the bandana that had become her signature look and her longer hair which she often wore tied back in a loose braid, hippie style, and the makeup all helped create the illusion that seventeen (almost eighteen) years-old Chiara Calvecchio, the runaway from Cairns, no longer existed.

Now she was 21-year-old Chiara DeRoma, a confident, experienced, and streetwise young woman, working in a hotel in West End, and living on a closed-in verandah with seven other young people, all of whom wanted to enjoy a free uncomplicated existence in a city that offered many opportunities.

There was only one problem, albeit a major one. It would be another three years before she was twenty-one so until then she needed to keep up the pretence and stay under the radar, away from the prying eyes of her family and the authorities.

She had written a letter home after her first month, making sure she mailed it from the other side of Brisbane.

'Dear parents,' she wrote. 'I am sorry I left without telling anybody. I could not face the thought of becoming a secretary and leaving as I did was the only way I could see to making my own future.

I am alright. I am not ready to tell you where I am, just that I am happy, I have a comfortable home and a job and I am safe. Please do not worry about me. I will write again soon.

Love Chiara."

Chapter Twenty-One

The following two years were an exciting whirlwind of work, fun, shopping, and parties. Chiara never imagined it could be possible to enjoy life in this way. She was proud of what she had achieved although she felt some shame about having to lie to get it.

Her small verandah room was getting smaller by the day as more furniture and decorations found their way there.

She loved the kaleidoscope of colours that were draped over her louvered windows and the fusion of bright colourful patterns everywhere. If she closed her eyes, she could hear the gypsies singing; their flutes and accordions playing. The air was filled with happy folk tunes as they danced around in her head.

She loved how her two blue budgerigars flew freely and would roost anywhere. Her room was their sanctuary and they were totally at home. They never wanted to escape to the outside world or from the large grey cat that sometimes found its way into her space. They loved to fly among the wild tangles of Devil's Ivy that grew lush in the life-giving morning light and humid afternoons.

Occasionally, she heard the other tenants clattering around in the kitchen, or the sound of the blowtorch as Sandra worked on her latest silver jewellery creations in the room next door. Sometimes the sound was different, especially when Sandra brought a man home, but it never lasted long. In the morning, he would be gone.

Life was good. Despite her merry-go-round of shopping, work almost every night and cleaning up after her birds, Chiara still found time to join in on the many house parties which was what the others called them. They would happen regularly. Spontaneously. Friends of the other housemates would wander in and strong, sometimes heated, political discussions and thoughts on what was wrong with the world would ensue.

Chiara would often come home from work to find her housemates in a haze of smoke, their friends lounging over scattered cushions, or sitting cross-legged on the floor, passing around a suspicious-smelling cigarette. They were all determined to change the world, one funny cigarette at a time.

Other times, she would arrive to a Bob Dylan tune on the record player and a roomful of trancelike dancers, swaying and spinning blissfully around the large common room and throwing their arms around her as she entered.

Sometimes, she joined them. At other times, she would walk through and sit on the back step, taking in the sounds inside with a wine in one hand and a cigarette in the other.

The drugs were offered occasionally but she always declined saying, "Life is enough of a high for me," but the truth was that drugs had never interested her.

She could not understand why people with such strong beliefs about the rampant social issues would dull their senses to the point that everything they said came out as a jumble of disjointed thoughts.

High on the political spectrum of discussions were freedom, war and peace. A common thread was that a solution was possible, but nobody in the group was determined to find it. All they ever did was talk about it which Chiara thought was strange. Maybe one day, they might take action?

Nevertheless, these young people were cool, calm, and fashionable, and Chiara felt totally in sync with their ideologies, even if they did not act on their beliefs.

Their lifestyle and mindset were having a huge impact on her own worldview and she was becoming quietly absorbed in issues that were important to her and her peers.

Life was colourful; life was fun; life had meaning, yet Chiara felt she was not close enough to them to immerse herself fully into their world. Instead, she was more than content to sit on the fringes and observe.

She listened intently, developed opinions based on her own observations, but always kept out of the discussions, never voicing her opinions, never offering solutions, and never feeling that she wanted to be a part of the change.

She could see it coming but she was not willing to be a part of it.

When someone would start strumming a guitar, she often experienced a twinge of nostalgia. She would lie back and be lulled by the soulful tunes, remembering when she and Tom were together and Tom would play his guitar.

Occasionally, someone would break into song, joining in the melody, but mostly, the 'singer' was so out of tune or off key that it sounded somewhere between a dying cat and a bellowing bull. These were the times Chiara would laugh softly and quietly retire to her room.

Her thoughts of Tom and the baby she gave away were few these days, but every now and then something would trigger a memory. A song on the radio, a smell, especially the jasmine at dusk in spring. It was the intoxicating scent that had wafted in the windows of the hostel the evening she began to bring Isabella into the world.

October memories would raise their head and tap her on the shoulder. Even now, with the sweet tones of Peter, Paul and Mary drifting into her room, she thought of that evening three years ago. Her memories were more indistinct but still raw and painful.

No-one ever saw the silent tears Chiara shed in October every year. It was her secret and her cross to bear as she wondered about her daughter. Was she happy? Was she talking yet? Was her hair red? There was a wound in her heart that would never be healed. It would always be there, deep in the recesses of her being.

Chapter Twenty-Two

B y May 1961, Bella was crawling. In September, she took her first steps.

Every milestone was a special event and her first birthday was marked by a celebration and a delicious chocolate cake, cooked and frosted by her mother and shared by many of the townspeople who came by for the occasion.

Gifts were plentiful, many of them practical like the bonnet and shoes to replace the ones she was growing out of but the one Bella was most excited about was the boy doll named 'George.' A companion to Faye, and Bella hugged them both.

Hand-sewn dolls clothes and a large cradle with tiny crocheted blankets were also wrapped in a parcel. Although Bella was still too young to be gentle, she cuddled them both tightly to her chest before dropping them into the cradle.

The first three years passed quickly. Before long, they were on a train to Sydney to collect Bella's grandparents off the boat from Italy. They couldn't wait to meet the little girl who had her Nonna's middle name. Bella was amazed by the big red buses; the double deckers she called mummy and daddy buses and the myriads of trams buzzing all over the city.

Finally, the ship arrived. Ava could not contain her excitement as she greeted her parents and little Bella bounced happily into her Nonna's arms, chattering non-stop about the traffic and the ducks on the river in the park. So much filled her mind and she needed to tell her brand new grandparents everything.

Nico and Ava laughed. Her chatter was delightful and nobody had any desire to stop it at all. This precious child could talk about anything she wanted and she had a captive audience in her parents and grandparents.

Fortunately, Ava and Nico spoke both English and Italian at home with Bella, so communication was not an issue with her grandparents who did not speak English. After two nights in Sydney, they travelled north. Ava's parents were surprised at the arid country that passed by the train window and they were even more shocked by the tiny station at Boggabilla and its ramshackle buildings. They were greeted by Judith and Doctor Jackson, and driven to the outback border town their daughter and son-in-law called home.

Their anxiety was quelled when they saw how beautiful Nico and Ava had made their little piece of paradise. Within days, they settled into rural Australian life and were beginning to love it, as Ava and Nico did.

It had been a long time since Nico heard any news about his family in Italy. It came as no surprise that his sister had married the son of a prestigious wine maker in the south and produced an heir last spring. Nico is relieved to hear that their elopement did not affect Ava's family at all and that they still worked in the vineyards and lived in the cottage in the town by the estate.

After all, Ava's father was too good a worker. He knew the vines too well. Nico's father knows that the grapes, and ultimately the wine, would be compromised if he lost the services of the long-time caretaker of the grapes. The Palladino vineyard is too well recognised to take such a big gamble.

It was sad news that the elderly cook and housekeeper had passed away after a short illness. Nico remembered her fondly. She had been a part of his life since childhood and he often dreamed of the wonderful treats she would serve the family after they feasted on risotto or a delicious lasagna. He longed for the sweet aroma of her homemade limoncello and vowed that one day he would learn the art so Bella could enjoy a small sweet taste of Italy when she was older.

Ava, though quite adept in the kitchen, had still not mastered the art of making a perfect panna cotta but her biscotti was becoming famous in the small town and her mother was proud.

That first night they enjoyed a simple minestrone with meatballs. The second night, and almost every night after, Sophia and her daughter would share the kitchen, and laugh and chop, and cook like the old days with Bella standing on her own stool to crack the eggs or pour the milk.

Ava was often transported back to a time when she was the one on the stool as her mother and Nonna prepared food for the family. Their raucous laughter, tender love and joyous happiness enriched every meal.

Having her mother with them was wonderful and she was eternally grateful that Bella had the opportunity to enjoy her Nonna like Ava did all those years ago. If she closed her eyes, she could hear the distant bells ringing in paddocks and the gentle bleating of the goats outside as they were herded for milking.

The time went too fast and January became May in the blink of an eye. In one more month, her parents would be returning in time for the Italian summer when the grapes ripen and the harvest begins. Her father took so much pride in his skills, and it was crucial he return before harvest. Only he knew how to select the best grapes for crushing.

Ava observed how much her father and mother adored their precious grandchild. During the days Nico was at work, Nonno and Bella worked on creating a doll's house for George and Faye who now has short spiky hair because Bella decided she needed a trim but did not understand that a doll's hair will never grow back. Nonna laughed at the doll's spiky haircut and it was decided that Faye needed a bonnet for her head.

Together, Bella and Nonna cut and shaped a scrap of fabric. While Bella slept, Nonna stitched the bonnet together, edging the plain white cotton with a trim of fine lace and finishing with a white satin ribbon. In the morning, Bella was excited as she dressed Faye in her new bonnet and sat her in the high chair with George, so that they could all share breakfast together.

The doll's house, with butterflies painted on the side, turned into a large two-story building that took up an entire corner of her bedroom. Beside it, the cradle for George and Faye to sleep in was polished with beeswax and every night Bella tucked them into bed before she settled down to listen to the stories of home told by her Nonna. Tales of forests and wandering gypsies, and fairies and elves that cast magical spells that ensured pleasant dreams for all children.

They loved spending time together in Ava and Nico's country home, taking long walks into town and by the river. They enjoyed time with the many friends who dropped by each morning for Ava's, and now also Sophia's, special biscotti. How they would miss the delicate but delicious panettone that Sophia baked for Easter.

When Sophia, Ava and Bella dropped by their homes, they were treated to the Australian delicacies of hot scones, fresh from the oven, laden with strawberry jam and cream. Sophia demanded the recipe for the deliciously spongy, chocolate and coconut covered, lamingtons. She wanted to recreate them at home for her own visitors back in Italy.

Their home for those five months was filled with a love that only a family can give, with aromas and comfort that only grandparents can provide. So, when the time came, all too soon, for them to head back to Sydney and board the ship for home, there were many tears and many hugs before they finally waved goodbye.

Life was sad and empty for a few days after they left, but Bella had the doll's house and many stories to remember them by. Every night, when she tucked George and Faye into their cradle, she said goodnight to Nonna and Nonno. She thought of them as she watched the butterflies painted on the sides of the doll house come to life and flutter in her dreams.

She hoped and wished for the day when she could see Nonna and Nonno again. She did not realise how far away Italy was, so, for now, her prayers of a reunion would remain unanswered.

Chapter Twenty-Three

Time moved rapidly. Chiara was now twenty years old. So many people have sat opposite her at the bar. So many people, so many stories, so much life around her.

Every night she heard a different story, told by a different person. Some interesting, some made her angry, and some even filled her with contempt. There were stories that left her with a burning desire to climb out of the little cocoon she had spun around herself, to spread her wings, and see more of the world. But for now, she had to be satisfied living vicariously through their travels which gave her glimpses of the world out there.

A world beyond Brisbane, beyond Cairns, beyond Rome, a world full of dancing. A world of high mountains and snow, or deep canyons and sandy deserts. She took it all in, imagining a fairytale existence in which she could transport herself magically to wherever she wants to be, whenever she wants to do it.

From her side of the bar, she was the listener. Sometimes, she secretly wished she could be the jury, or someone handing down a sentence, sometimes even the executioner. She seethed at the tales about bad marriages, unhappy men, wives they married but did not love, men who needed something or someone else. She hears it all.

When she saw a man with a woman she knew wasn't his wife, or worse, when he begins to flirt with her, she remembered the gypsy creed: never judge someone because they sin differently to you. These were the times she moved away. It was hard but she reminded herself that it was not her place to judge anybody. She learnt a long time ago that, when you cast stones at others, they bounced back and hit you twice as hard. 'After all, I'm not without sin myself,' she thought.

She was becoming cynical, however, and beginning to grow weary of the same pattern, night after night after night. Sad men, bitter men, angry men, men with wives who would nag, wives who were too tired to be wives, wives they did not find attractive anymore, or men who had never loved their wives but who, for reasons they couldn't explain, married them anyway.

Occasionally, younger single men frequented the hotel. Their reasons were as varied as the men themselves. Every now and then, one of them would pique her interest, but she became bored when, after a few drinks, they told her about their sad lives or the girl they wanted who didn't want them. Men drowning their sorrows with alcohol or using Chiara as a way to unburden their tortured souls.

She was not interested, having lived through this trauma in her youth. She witnessed the impact it had on Tom and his family and felt the burden of providing comfort. She felt the sting of abandonment by her own family when she needed them most and the grief of having what was most precious to her, her child, forcibly taken from her, never to be seen or spoken of ever again.

In the years she was alone, she built a protective shell around herself, and was determined that no man was ever going to penetrate it again. The hurt was too great.

Lately, a lot more overseas servicemen were calling the hotel home. Many simply wanted to drink and hang out with their friends, and enjoy being young men in another country. However, some of them wanted a friendly face to reassure them that they were not so alone in this strange new country.

This particular night, the bar was full. A ship had disembarked, their officers and crew were on rec leave. Most of them chose her hotel to let their hair down.

She listened to the happy chatter and dreamy tales of faraway lands as they talked excitedly amongst themselves.

"They have been to so many places," she mused from the other side of the bar, absent-mindedly wiping a glass as she watched and listened.

Drink after drink flowed, and as their glasses emptied, their inhibitions melted away. Occasional scuffles broke out at the pool table but were resolved when the publican stepped in. As the night progressed, they became merrier. Men in uniform, laughing, breaking into song, and encouraging the whole bar to join in. One young man needed to be coaxed down from a table and another from the bar.

Some stumbled and slurred and their stories became a jumbled mess of memories with no clear timeline. Others became angry, developing a false bravado that eventually caused their ejection from the bar. They staggered onto the night street. Men with drunken gaits were strung out along the footpath all the way to where their ship was berthed.

Toward the end of the night, a small number remained. They were unchanged, still sober, no matter how much beer they had drunk.

That was why she was surprised when she saw the non-uniformed stranger at the end of the bar, sitting alone and staring at the space in front of him. 'Islander maybe?' she thought, dark olive skin like herself, but a big man with big hair. Long ringlets bounced to his shoulders; he was unshaven and slightly unkempt.

He sat there silently, a glass of rum his only friend. 'Different,' she thought, 'Most men here prefer beer.' She was fascinated, and her head tilted slightly as she tried to read his features.

He looked up and caught her gaze. She quickly looked away, embarrassed at being caught, but she was intrigued. She stole another glance.

He smiled, and there was something in his eyes that was mesmerizing. He was an enigma.

Swallowing the last of his rum in one gulp, he held his empty glass up to call her over.

"Well, you are a pretty little thing," he said when she came over to refill his glass.

"Thank you," she answered but not with the usual confidence that braced her for the 'wife at home' story that nearly always followed.

"Where does that accent come from?" he asked genuinely interested.

"Italy," she replied, "I came here with my parents seven years ago," and she instantly pulled herself up, realising she had almost revealed her true age. "Sorry, it was actually 10 years ago now, I seem to have lost track of time."

He smiled knowingly. He was not fooled for an instant, but he really didn't care about her age. There was something special about her that he couldn't define. If he read the signs correctly, she felt the same way about him.

"Hi, Italy girl, I'm Martin."

"Where are you from, Martin?" she asked, also detecting a slight accent.

"New Zealand."

"Why are you in Australia, Martin?"

"Not a lot of work in New Zealand, so I thought I'd try my luck here," and added "What about you, are your parents still in Brisbane?"

Chiara did not know what to say, she wanted to be honest, she felt drawn to this stranger but she had never told anyone the truth about her. Nobody knew that she had run away at almost 18, that her home was in Cairns, not Brisbane, and that she had been working all this time in the hotel as a minor. She needed to think of a story and fast.

"My parents are in Sydney," she said. "I came here for a change of pace and never left." It was sort of true, she thought.

He was suspicious, but satisfied. He knew she had a story and she would share it when and if she chose to. He emptied his glass and pushed it forward for a refill. His eyes were still clear and his voice remained unchanged, not even slightly slurred.

Chiara was impressed. A man who holds his liquor is a rare man indeed and this one had not changed at all even after drinking almost a third of a bottle of overproof rum. It was a slow night after most of the servicemen had left. Chiara was able to chat with the stranger at the bar while she carried out her duties.

She learnt all about New Zealand, the mountains and oceans that sounded so pristine and wild. From the way he talked, Chiara could tell Martin had a love-and-hate relationship with his country. He did not speak about his family and Chiara did not ask. She formed the impression there was a lot of tension and she knew how that felt.

His gaze when he spoke to her was intense. No one had ever held her so captivated. She felt drawn to his strong masculine features and fought the impulse to reach out and touch his deep olive skin. His dark eyes were a window into his inner thoughts and she couldn't take her eyes away from his. She was struggling against a riptide but it felt so good.

They talked about music and performers, such as Dylan and The Band, the Beatles, and the strange hold they had on the teenagers, about Joni Mitchell and the Animals, and how performers became performing artists, how the music was about protests, about all the things wrong in the world and where the world was heading.

They talked about how big changes were coming. But what they were, and what it would mean, they didn't know. All they knew for sure was this young 1960s generation was restless and dissatisfied. Like the song, 'The times, they are a changing.'

Chiara realised she had talked more in these hours with this stranger about social issues, music and politics than she had in the last two years with any of her housemates. Something felt familiar to her: it was a closeness that comes from a connection of minds and souls. She had felt this before with Tom, but had been too young to understand it. Even after so short a time, she and Martin were soulmates, linked one to the other in some mysterious, hypnotic way.

Chiara was finally letting her guard down. A force stronger than her own will had taken over her entire being. She was in a trance. Addicted to the drug that was him, she couldn't release herself from his magnetism.

This hadn't happened since Tom and it frightened her.

Martin was a big man, almost twice her weight and over a foot taller, but she sensed a gentleness in him. When he smiled at her, his entire face lit up. Huge bulky muscles bulged under his checked shirt, and he looked fierce when he widened his eyes and flared his nostrils which Chiara found all the more intoxicating.

When the hotel closed that night, and her shift was over, she could not say goodbye to him. She needed this man with her. Walking home together, she took his hand and lifted his arm to her shoulder. She needed to feel his strong arms around her, his lips on hers and his body against her. She brought him to her room and he proved to be a very tender, gentle lover who awakened parts of her body she hadn't realised existed. Even with Tom, she had not felt so alive.

He stayed till noon, then was back at the hotel the next night, and the night after that, joining her always at her home afterwards. They were deeply infatuated and their desire for each other was undeniably intense. Their relationship was like an inferno which burned out of control when they were together and smouldered gently in the afterglow.

She eventually told him the truth (or some of it) about her life, how she left Italy under a shroud of secrecy, not knowing and not caring about what her parents were running from. How they had arrived in Cairns, and how, after four years, she left Cairns at seventeen to study at Secretarial School. But she decided against it right before her eighteenth birthday, and ended up working at the hotel instead.

She revealed how she lied about her age, and how she was not yet twenty-one and still considered a runaway. She told him she worried that, if her secret was exposed, there would be serious consequences.

He listened without judgement, and told her he had no family left in New Zealand. His grandmother with whom he lived for most of his life had passed away after a short illness early last year. Her death was what convinced him to explore more about what his life might have to offer.

Nothing bound him to New Zealand anymore. No close family, the country was in deep recession and work was hard to find. Everything was getting really expensive. It was time to try life somewhere else.

"So many Kiwis talked about Australia and that getting here was easy," he said. "I hopped on a boat and, three days later, boom, I was here."

She never mentioned Tom, or the time in the hostel when Isabella was born. That part of her life was over, a painful memory that couldn't be changed. Telling him served no purpose, and she didn't want to share it with anyone anyway, not even Martin.

For four months, she was in a blissful trance. Long passionate nights and deep, meaningful days. Life with Martin was a dream she didn't want to wake up from.

January 1964, it was a morning just like every other morning. Chiara woke as usual, wiped the sleep from her eyes and looked at Martin in the early morning sunlight. His powerful arms held her protectively against him in the tiny single bed, their bodies intertwined as one.

A calm contentment swept over her as she traced the outline of his muscles with her fingertips, marvelling at how strong they were and how gentle they felt.

Without warning, a wave of nausea overcame her and as she lifted his arm to be able to slide down and out of the bed. She also felt a slight hardening and swelling in her breasts and a tingling in her nipples.

In that moment, she was completely awake, realising what these symptoms meant. Ignoring them would be futile, this couldn't be ignored away, Isabella was living proof of that.

Returning from the bathroom, her fears were confirmed by the tightening of her jeans as she buttoned them up, this could only mean one thing. That life with Martin was about to change. The carefree existence they had enjoyed up until now would soon be a thing of the past.

Martin took the news well and he kissed her swelling abdomen as they discussed what the next step in their lives would be.

It was a brief ceremony. Chiara wore a pale blue shift to conceal her ballooning midriff, and a white shawl to protect her shoulders from the biting wind that gripped Brisbane that winter. They married in May 1964, exactly one month after her 21st birthday, at the local courthouse with Ross and Veronica from the share house as witnesses.

Chiara and Martin stood before the Justice of the Peace, exchanged vows and rings, kissed, said thank you to Ross and V. They stepped into the wind to catch a tram back to West End to begin packing away her old life and beginning the new.

Saying goodbye to her verandah room was hard, as was leaving the hotel that had been her life for the last two and a half years. The publican hugged her and wished them well. She wiped a silent tear as she packed the final scarf into a box and watched as Martin and Ross, a fellow Kiwi, carried the last of her furniture and boxes to the trailer to be moved to their new cottage on the other side of Brisbane. A tiny brick and fibro box with an overgrown yard close to the Ports where Martin had managed to pick up some seasonal work.

Chiara experienced the same sensations of emptiness and abandonment that had washed over her at the hostel all those years ago. Slowly, the life she had built and was proud of dissolved around her. She wasn't sure when or how it started, only that the fire was no longer burning as brightly. The dream was finally over and life was becoming a harsh reality.

Two months later, noticeably pregnant and feeling lost and lonely, Chiara looked around the sparse room and then at the blank page on the table in front of her. It had been well over two years since the last letter to her parents. It had been brief, a short outline letting them know she was OK and not to worry about her. This letter was far more. This time she was telling them that her life had changed. She was married, and within a few months they would become grandparents.

"Everything is going well, there are no problems with the pregnancy, and the baby is due somewhere near the end of August," she wrote. She changed her mind and scrunched the paper into a ball, tossing it angrily onto the growing pile of rejected drafts.

"Why is this so hard?" she said out loud to the empty room as she tore another sheet from the writing pad.

"*Dear parents*" she started.

"I'm sorry it has been a long time since I wrote last. Life has been very busy, and as time went by, I found it harder and harder to find the time. I wasn't sure if you ever wanted to hear from me again."

'Well, that bit is the truth,' she said to herself.

"I have been working at a respectable place, serving meals and cleaning, and I had a wonderful little room of my own in a house that I shared with several other people, mostly university students."

She looked at the page, ready to add it to the rejects pile but decided the time for reconciliation was well overdue. "I need to do this," she told herself, and continued putting her thoughts onto the paper.

"In the last year, my life has changed. I met a wonderful man, named Martin Williams. He is from New Zealand but living here now and he has a job on the wharves near where we are living. We love each other very much and in May we got married." She stopped for a minute and stared at the page. It read like a manuscript, not a heartfelt letter to her parents, but this time she was determined to get it finished. Tapping the biro on the table, she collected her thoughts before deciding what to write next.

Feeling the baby move, she readjusted herself on the uncomfortable vinyl dining chair whilst absently caressing her swollen tummy, feeling the baby move around underneath her hand. "OK, little one, I get the message, I will tell them about you."

"Mama & Papa, there is more news that I need to share with you. We are expecting a baby sometime at the end of August or early September. He or she is very restless and

moving around right now, especially since I started writing this letter. I think the baby wants to hurry up and get here so that he or she can meet Nonna & Nonno.

"My health is good and everything is progressing well with the pregnancy and Martin and I are very excited." Our home is small but comfortable. We are renting a cottage; you will find the address on the back of this envelope. We don't have a lot of furniture yet as we haven't been married very long but we are getting more and more as time goes on. Each week we use money from Martin's pay to buy the things we need for the baby and the nursery is starting to look very nice."

That's not totally true, she thought, but it did have a bassinette and some baby clothes. They were planning to buy a cot from the second-hand store very soon.

She glanced around at the dining room she was sitting in. Again, her scarves covered the windows and the scant furniture from her verandah room was placed randomly around the lounge and in their bedroom. They had managed to purchase a small table and chairs, a very heavy refrigerator and a double bed from the thrift store. Ross and V gave them some cutlery, crockery and two saucepans from the house in West End. V was sure they wouldn't be missed, along with the cushions from the lounge room which she and Chiara had placed on top of some wooden boxes that were covered with an old cotton sheet Martin brought home. Not exactly fine furniture but it became a passable lounge that would suffice until they could buy a real one.

Chiara missed the bohemian look of her old verandah room. Even though she used the same things, she could not recreate the same look and feel. Maybe because it was so much bigger than her verandah, but Chiara hated how hollow and empty the house sounded when they talked. 'Never mind,' she thought, 'it will fill up quickly and be a home once the baby arrives.' But she failed to convince herself.

Snapping back to the letter in front of her, she finished it by emphasising how happy she was, and how content she felt with her life and how she was anxiously awaiting the baby's arrival.

"If it's a boy, I might like to call him Jacob and if it's OK with you, Papa, I should like to give your name as his middle name." They had discussed a girl's name and settled on Susanna, but they had not decided on a middle name but she told them that if it was a girl then the middle name should be Calvecchio, that way she will have her Italian heritage forever, even when she is grown up and married." She reread the letter and was satisfied.

Folding it up, she placed it in the envelope and popped it in the mailbox on the footpath outside. "No turning back now," she said as she walked back. A tangle of weeds sprouted from what was once a flower bed along the old wire fence. She imagined how it would have looked before it was so neglected.

Fleetingly, a memory of a much younger Chiara wandering the streets of Fremantle came to mind and the blade of grass that made everything make sense.

One delicate iris blossom was raising its head above the weeds.

Chiara watched as a beautiful red and black butterfly settled on the iris, fanning its wings before fluttering along the path in front of her.

It flew off before she entered the house, but somehow it felt significant to her. She thought of the gypsies and how every animal had a reason for their existence. A butterfly indicated a direction that must be followed, the path to a new beginning. The restless baby moved once more as if agreeing she was indeed on the right path forward.

Chapter Twenty-Four

They arrived in late August 1964. Enzo spent the last two weeks of Chiara's pregnancy doing repairs inside and taming the garden of the run-down cottage to ensure it was in the best possible condition for their grandchild.

September chased the cold away and the weather was becoming balmy. Gina sat on the top step of the front patio, busily knitting, Chiara sat on a kitchen chair, with the patio rail beside her, her cumbersome body making it difficult to do anything quickly.

Enzo was in the midday sun pulling weeds from the overgrown garden beds. "So many flowers," thought Chiara, far more than she realised. All through winter, the garden was a tangled mess of creeping ivy and thistles, but now what a difference. Tall flower heads were pushing their way through the weeds and reaching for the early spring sunlight.

Chiara was astonished at how much nicer the yard looked after receiving a little attention from her father. She wondered how much more could be hidden beneath the rampant ferns and vines that ran alongside the steps and patio. In her imagination, she saw a perfect cottage garden lining the pathway and framing the small front patio.

In her mind's eye, she could see herself sitting there in the morning sun and watching her child play. In the afternoon, they would sit together as they waited for Martin to come home from work. It truly was a wonderful dream.

Labour came on suddenly, pulling her out of her daydream, more suddenly than before and, as in her first pregnancy, her waters broke. Gina stayed by her side while Enzo ran to get Martin from work. A taxi arrived soon after.

The pain wasn't so bad yet and she knew she had a while to wait, although the hospital wasn't that far away.

Martin was like every other brand new, expectant father and by the time they arrived at the hospital he was an anxious mess.

Chiara was surprisingly calm, he thought, not knowing that it wasn't her first time giving birth. Nobody except her parents knew, not even her doctor, so it wasn't surprising the nurses treated her like an inexperienced first-time mother.

Martin was told to go home, or at least wait outside, as there were no visitors allowed until after the baby was born.

Chiara yelped as a stronger pain gripped her body. This was the nurse's cue. She was told to say goodbye to Martin, she hugged him tightly before being ushered into a small room across the corridor. She was put on a bed, prepped and pushed down another long corridor through a curtain on the other side. All along the walls were glossy green cubicles that had no doors, only curtains and a high bed in each.

Several curtains were closed and she could hear the moaning of at least two other women in various stages of labour.

Once in her own cubicle, the curtain was drawn, and she was left alone. She thought about how different this experience was from her last.

Nurses looked in occasionally to check her progress but they rarely spoke. Eventually, sometime later in the evening, a doctor arrived and her legs were hoisted up into stirrups over either side of the bed. It all felt very undignified. She couldn't remember this part of her labour when giving birth to Isabella.

A sheet had been pulled across her middle like a curtain and a mask was put over her face. It became a hazy blur afterwards. The only thing she remembered was the horrible taste from the mask as she inhaled deeply, and the strange sensation of hovering somewhere above the bed as Isabella slid into the world.

Without the assistance of gas this time, she was painfully aware of everything. Sometime before dawn, Jacob Lorenzo Williams was born.

He was a healthy 9lb 4oz, a sturdy little fellow, with deep olive skin, a mop of black curls and an incredibly strong set of lungs. When she saw him, she remarked how much he resembled his father.

She was given five catgut stitches, checked over to ensure everything was where it was meant to be and cleaned up.

Jacob was left in her arms in the postnatal ward until her breakfast arrived, after which the nurse returned him to the nursery The nurse offered her a cigarette which she accepted. She watched the rising of the sun from her window. The hospital was very strict about visitors. Parents and friends could visit from 2 p.m. to 4 p.m., and 6 p.m. to 8 p.m. was reserved for the fathers.

Gina spent the afternoon with her daughter and was smitten when she first held her grandson.

Martin and Enzo waited in the public bar across the road with several other new dads whilst Gina visited first. The two men arrived that first night a little tipsy and very merry. It made Chiara laugh as she remembered her younger days and her happy but drunken father in the hotel each night in Rome.

She never had trouble finding him as he was always the one with the loudest laugh and would be surrounded by equally merry patrons. She would tug on his shirt and feel like a princess when he lifted her high in the air and spun her around, telling everyone to say hello to his beautiful daughter. She would laugh and remind him that Mama had a lasagne ready and he had to come home now otherwise it would be fed to the street dogs.

He always did, but not before downing one last drink, laughing at one last joke and fondly embracing his friends before leaving with tiny Chiara on his shoulders, promising to be back the next day or maybe the day after.

The hospital staff were not impressed. Martin and Enzo were ordered out, but not before they visited the nursery and waved happily to little Jacob through the large plate glass window.

Chiara was happy that her father and husband were getting along so well, but she felt very disempowered by the entire process.

She wanted to spend more time with her baby. For the three weeks she was there, she was only able to see him during the mothercraft lessons, changing nappies, bathing him and learning how to breastfeed properly. She felt a pang of fear every time he was taken back to the nursery.

Each morning, everyone had to stay in bed until the ward was cleaned and inspected by the matron. Chiara found it amusing that everyone was allowed to smoke, including the visitors, and the cleaners could never get rid of the nauseating smell of smoke.

The rest of her days consisted of chatting with other mothers about their dreamy home lives and wonderful husbands, or wandering the halls in search of company or something to break the monotony or relaxing and reflecting in the hospital garden. Several of the more experienced mothers were happy to impart their knowledge, sometimes helpful, but mostly fuelled by their frustration at the thankless role of motherhood.

Chiara and two other brand-new mothers, as wide eyed and bewildered as she was, listened as they chatted incessantly about the constant merry-go-round of nappies, washing, cooking, cleaning, sleepless nights and squabbling children and never having time to do what they enjoyed any longer. Even relaxing for ten minutes with a hot cup of tea was a luxury for some of them.

They painted a picture of motherhood as a 24/7 series of chores with no respite and no recognition or thanks. 'No wonder old ladies are often bitter and cranky,' she thought. Like every other idealistic new parent, she told herself, 'My life won't be like that because I have a good husband who will be helpful and my child will be happy and well behaved.'

"At least I am well looked after," she said to her mother during her afternoon visit at the beginning of her second week. "They are teaching me how to take care of my baby, and he is doing well but it is really hurting when I feed him myself. "She put her hand over her cracked nipple that had started to scab over from where it was bleeding. Breastfeeding was becoming a very painful experience but she was not ready to give up yet.

She had an irrational fear that, if she was to stop feeding him herself, something or someone would take this baby away from her. Illogically, she believed he would stay with her if he was reliant on her for sustenance. She didn't share this fear with anyone, of course, but it frightened her enough to invade her dreams at night. She would wake up in a cold sweat and have to check the nursery to make sure he was still there.

The fear also made it difficult to feel secure enough to develop any strong feelings for Jacob. She loved him but was afraid that, if she connected to him as a mother should, the pain would be unbearable if he was taken away from her.

After ten days the stitches were removed, and she endured stinging salt baths until the healing was complete. She didn't remember this much physical pain with Isabella but of course, Isabella was much smaller and was never breast fed. At that dreadful time, the only pain was in her heart and from having to express the milk glands daily for relief.

Jacob Lorenzo came home after three weeks and Chiara was surprised at how much her parents had accomplished while she was in hospital. His nursery was still stark, but comfortable with new white linen curtains on the windows and a small single day bed against the far wall beside the large dark timber cot. All the cushions from the loungeroom were now on the bed. A simple timber cupboard was positioned against the wall and a small rug was on the linoleum floor.

Chiara wondered where people would now sit at night, but when she joined the others, she noticed a large green sofa and a new floor mat now filled the space where her makeshift 'milkcrate' sofa had been. Her bright orange furniture from her West End room had pride of place as a separator between the dining and lounge areas.

A larger table with six orange vinyl covered chairs graced the dining area and the smaller table and two chairs it replaced were in the entry area under the patio window and served as a writing desk.

A large black kettle replaced the saucepan they had used to boil water on the wood stove. The kitchen boasted new timber shelves on the wall above the bench with a new matching crockery set, a biscuit jar and new cookware. A set of pretty glasses with delicate gold stars was arranged along the shelf of a simple timber hutch.

At that moment, it dawned on her that being a parent was far more than giving birth. It involved unconditional love, adversity, strength, resilience and, no matter how much a child rejected their parents as she had done, there was forgiveness.

With tears in her eyes and a new-found wisdom, she walked over and embraced them both, thanking them for everything they had done for her, not only at this time, but also through her life. Chiara felt she was finally growing up and ready to enter the next phase of her life.

Her father returned to Cairns several days later, the family wishing him a safe trip as he stepped into the taxi to take him to the train station.

Gina, besotted by Jacob and his adorable crop of glossy black curls, dark complexion, and eyes that made her melt every time she held him, decided to stay for another month. Martin would leave for work early in the morning and come home late in the evening.

For a while, life was bliss.

With her mother's help over those first few weeks, Chiara settled easily into motherhood and domestic life. She still had anxieties about losing Jacob so her instinct was to keep him close and never to allow anyone to come close enough to take him while she wasn't looking. She didn't notice the toll this was having on Martin as he slowly became more and more distant. The change was so gradual that it went unnoticed at first.

The longer absences from home, the later returns from work, even the slight smell of alcohol on his breath and smoke on his clothing were missed by the women as they were totally absorbed by tiny Jacob. But Martin was feeling rejected, pushed out of his home, his marriage and no longer needed or wanted.

He reacted by leaving even earlier for work, walking instead of taking a tram, and sitting in a hotel in the evenings, coming home late at night, often too tired to eat and barely acknowledging his wife or infant son as he walked through the cottage. He would collapse, unkempt and fully dressed onto the bed, falling asleep without waiting for Chiara to join him.

While she was reluctant to allow anyone to hold her son, Chiara encouraged Martin to at least touch their baby boy. But he always had a reason not to. She was perplexed. A man as loving and gentle as he had been at the start of their relationship was now a stranger who was becoming more distant as each day passed.

Chiara knew that something 'wasn't quite right' anymore. What was happening to them?

At night, in the privacy of their bedroom, they would argue quietly so as not to disturb Gina or the baby sleeping in the next room.

When she went to touch him in bed, he would recoil, saying he was too tired and needed to sleep. When he rolled over and feigned sleep, he was secretly hoping she would reach out and touch him again anyway. He ached to be a real father; he desperately wanted her touch but she was simultaneously pushing him away and pulling him back.

On the one hand, she wanted him to be a part of their lives but, on the other, she acted as if he wasn't welcome. He couldn't understand why everything had changed. His emotions were a scrambled mess. Jacob had claimed her heart and soul and Martin was feeling the cutting edge of rejection.

Like Martin, Chiara was conflicted. The pain in her heart was sharp. She would look at him and feel love but, when he was distant and wouldn't speak to her or hold their baby, it frightened her. Where did he go? Who was this stranger? Why does he hate me so much?

The piercing screams from the baby next door would push all thoughts from her mind. She was not aware that Jacob had her full undivided attention: that every ounce of feeling, every gentle touch, every word of comfort she had left was given to him.

Chiara knew that this time her baby would not be taken away from her, but a raw instinct compelled her to hold him close and not let him go. The rational part of her mind told her to stop worrying, that Jacob was legally her baby, but a deep illogical fear gripped her and wouldn't let go. If Jacob was entrusted to anybody else, she would never see him again. It was a painful loss she could not go through again.

But how could she explain this to Martin? She didn't understand it herself. Martin didn't know about Isabella or that period in her life, so how could he ever understand her fears?

Chapter Twenty-Five

Two months after arriving, Gina reluctantly departed, leaving Chiara, Martin and baby Jacob alone. Somehow, they needed to come together as a family, find a way to bridge the gulf between them and reignite the spark that brought them together in the first place. Past lovers trying to find a way back to each other.

Chiara feared it was too late. They had become strangers, ships in the night passing each other, sleeping in the same house but barely acknowledging the other's presence.

She tried cooking his favourite meals, but he was rarely home to eat them. Wearing his favourite cologne, putting on makeup before he came home, acting provocatively after Jacob was asleep, but nothing. Not even a glimmer. There was no bridge and the gulf was widening.

Their relationship became a deep ravine, a bottomless pit and neither was able to see things from the other side. All they understood was what they were feeling, and that was pain, confusion, frustration, and rejection. It was only words as they talked 'at' each other; there was no listening, no feeling, no empathy. Emptiness. The void was an echo chamber where they felt unheard, unloved, unwanted and unable to find a way back.

The reality of how far their relationship had sunk could no longer be ignored or denied. Their conversations were stilted and tense and would often explode into a volatile argument. The same passion that brought them together was now fuelling their anger and driving them apart.

Their life became a merry-go-round of conflict. Small disagreements escalated rapidly and their raised voices became a cacophony of angry words. It was just noise and they were not prepared to acknowledge the other's reasons for feeling the way they did. The truth was, they didn't know the other's reasons. All they felt was smouldering pain and resentment.

It was early morning and they didn't even know what they were arguing about.

"Chiara, stop! .... I can't take this anymore!"

Martin's shoulders slumped in defeat as he stormed out of the house, slamming the front door behind him She watched from the window as he walked up the pathway and out of sight.

She hoped he wouldn't come back but felt terribly guilty at the same time. 'How much of it was her fault? She was sad to think that her son would either grow up with an absent father or if they stayed together his childhood would be like a war zone.

"Maybe if I tried a bit harder, stopped being angry, tried to talk to him more?" she wracked her brain over it but she had already tried them all. Nothing worked! Their relationship had died.

Martin did come back that night but soon after he began disappearing for days at a time. Chiara was no stranger to being alone, but being alone and caring for a baby was a whole new concept. It was hard.

Daily rituals had become a chore, there was nobody to dress up for, no reason to wear makeup or cologne. Meals for one were a bother to cook. The house was kept clean and tidy but the home Chiara had been creating with her new family was dissolving in front of her eyes.

Her world was imploding all over again. Not because someone else was controlling it, not because she was being forced to live in a way she resented, not because she was being pushed to take a direction she did not want or like. This time it was her own doing; her life was in a mess and it was her own fault. .

Occasionally, Martin did come home, but he was unkempt, dirty and barely spoke.

Chiara took to sleeping on the daybed in Jacob's room and Martin would sleep on the sofa in the lounge room. The big double bed, in the room that held all their past hopes and dreams, was untouched. Neither of them entered that room ever again.

Some mornings she would wake to an empty house and find his pay packet on the kitchen table then he wouldn't be seen again for another few days. At least he still cared enough to ensure his family was financially taken care of.

Chiara admired him for being responsible. Regardless of the home situation, however, Jacob grew to be a sweet and loving child. His laughter and smiles would light up a room.

But that sweetness was tempered with a feisty determined nature, a legacy inherited from both his parents. When he cried, he was a little bellowing bull and could not be ignored. He had a way of creasing his brow and pursing his lips that commanded attention.

For such a small person, he made a huge impact and, unlike his parents, he refused to go unnoticed.

As Jacob became more demanding of his mother's attention, Chiara became less aware of Martin's comings and goings. She reached the point where she was numb, having fallen out of love with Martin. Her life revolved about her and her child. There was no room for Martin.

Jacob was six months old when Martin told her that he needed to leave indefinitely. In his hand was an official letter from the New Zealand Government. He had four weeks to get all his affairs in order and leave Australia. He had been called up for military service in his home country.

He explained to Chiara how in New Zealand legally all males must register on their 20th birthday for compulsory military training with the Department of Labour. He had actually done that long before he left but because he lived in Australia and it was such a long time ago, he forgot about it. The system was that ballots decided who would undertake compulsory service and his name had recently been drawn.

He was required to complete three months' full-time
training in New Zealand, followed by an annual com-
mitment of part-time training over three years, with the
possibility of being drafted into service during that time.
He was required to return to his country to fulfill his duty.

Chiara didn't argue. She knew the marriage was over
and this situation was simply pushing forward the inevitable. Martin made one last attempt at reaching out
to Chiara by saying that the New Zealand army offered
passage for wives and children from Australia to New
Zealand. If he enlisted into active service, a home would
be provided for them by the army.

This prospect had no appeal to Chiara. She didn't want
to start again in yet another foreign country. She didn't
care to be surrounded by strangers, in a strange country
with a new baby, and a man who didn't love her anymore
and whom she no longer loved.

She didn't have to think about it, the choice was simple.
She would stay here and he would continue to support
them financially from wherever he may be in the future.

Everything happened very quickly following that discussion. Martin left, Jacob started crawling, then walking and
Chiara settled into her new role as a solo mother with
an absent partner. Being a mother with no husband to
support her was challenging. There were nights when a
partner would have eased the physical demands of a growing child and allowed her to enjoy a much-needed sleep

when he was crying from teething pain, or had a childhood fever that kept her awake and worrying all night.

She experienced the inevitable bouts of loneliness that came with being confined to a home and caring for a young child. There was no social interaction other than doctor's visits, vaccinations and the occasional storekeeper chats about how fast he was growing or the continual need for new clothing, shoes, a stroller as the pram became far too small and he was too little to walk very far on his own.

The cheques continued to arrive like clockwork and during the early stages while Jacob was still very young, they didn't want for anything. Life was mundane, but in settled kind of way.

To the outside world, her status as a single mother was due to external circumstance but, inwardly, she knew the truth. It was divine intervention and everything was playing out the way it was meant to. The only direction now was forward.

Socially, it was much more acceptable to tell others that her husband was in service, not that he had deserted her and their marriage was over. But still, she was restless. There was a gap she couldn't fill and her soul craved something more but she didn't have a clue what it was.

The amount Martin sent covered the rent, bought them food and paid the utilities and anything left went towards other expenses. She was becoming quite the manager of household finances, however, there was never any money left for a social life or luxuries.

For the first five months, the cheques arrived regularly, then she received word that he was being sent to war in Asia.

In the following months, the cheques arrived from Malaysia, Singapore, and finally Vietnam. Occasionally, a letter would accompany the cheque. Martin described the camp and his fellow soldiers. He complained about the humidity and constant problems with mosquitos or the occasional outbreaks of malaria and other tropical diseases. Thankfully, he managed to stay healthy himself whilst others were laid up for weeks in army hospital beds.

For over a year, Chiara and Jacob survived month to month on the frugal cheques she received from Vietnam, but then the letters stopped arriving so she knew nothing of his whereabouts or when he would be returning. Communication with the New Zealand army was very difficult, so she had to wait until a letter arrived from either Martin or the army itself.

She knew that, as there was no relationship in Australia to return to, after Vietnam he would probably stay in New Zealand. She would face that when it happened. There was no point pondering or making plans at the present time.

Jacob was a toddler now, running everywhere, talking constantly, and asking often about his brave soldier father and his whereabouts.

Because he was still an infant when his father left, his only memories were those created by his mother. So every evening when she tucked Jacob into bed, she told him fanciful stories of the exciting life his father was having.

Jacob listened attentively, eyes glowing with pride at his brave father's wonderful adventures. Chiara told her son, "Your Dad can't wait to come home, sit you on his knee and tell you lots of stories about his amazing life and all the places and animals he's seen."

So, Chiara continued nightly with the tales of jungles and forests filled with cheeky monkeys, friendly tigers and a superhero dad who was away saving the world. In this way, Jacob remained mesmerized and comforted by the image he built of his Dad who lived in a jungle way over the other side of the ocean.

Chapter Twenty-Six

It was the end of 1964. Tom went on a rare night out to herald the New Year. After all, in six weeks, all his hard work would be behind him and his apprenticeship completed.

He cut a lonely figure, sitting quietly amongst the revellers, under the downstairs awning of his local hotel. With semi-interest, he watched the Story Bridge and the twinkling lights on the Brisbane River. All around him, people waited excitedly for the countdown to midnight to begin, but Tom drifted into his own reflection of the last four years and the course his life had taken since leaving Cairns.

News from home had become sporadic. Patrick still wrote occasionally although the letters were not as regular as they used to be.

He was pleased to hear that Mary had finally settled into a kind of normality. Patrick wrote that she had attracted the attentions of a gentleman caller who was visiting lately.

Patrick wrote: *'It must be special, because she has been cooking and cleaning a lot, and even wears her best church dress in the middle of the week.'* Tom chuckled when he read that sentence. He couldn't imagine his mother dressing up for anyone except the church, and that was only on Sundays.

The twins went back home a year ago, I think the Wallaces finally gave up because they are still as wild as ever. 'She doesn't really bother with them too much,' wrote Patrick. 'They spend a lot of time away from home anyway. I think they are into a bit of mischief. Not sure what they get up to.'

Irene's birthday went well. Mother baked a cake and put eight candles on it and we all had a bit of a party at home. It felt good to be a normal family for a while and the cake was actually pretty tasty.'

Tom felt an emotional tug at that news of the family gathering, and was happy the family was finally starting to heal.

'We hardly ever hear from Jimmy these days, although I can tell you he has left Townsville and is now working on a trawler up near Cooktown. He drops in every few months to let us know he is still alive. He seems happy enough and looks alright, but does not stay long.'

Patrick wrote about the cyclone that hit them a few years ago and how it caused more damage to the house than was initially thought. *'As a result, it had taken a lot longer to fix the roof damage. Water that we didn't notice caused a problem underneath and the floor is a bit wonky. I'm trying to clean up the yard, it's like a jungle now.'*

Memories flooded back when he read how the shed at the back had to be completely demolished as the damage was too severe. He thought about the times he spent in that room escaping from the chaotic world around him and how his only comfort was when Chiara was in his arms.

The memories were vivid, but the pain was long gone. These days, the memories felt like they belonged to a bad dream from which he had long since woken. For years he felt totally desensitized, but he slowly healed. Eventually, he felt his soul coming back to life after its deep sleep.

The removal of the shed was a sign. That chapter in his early years was at an end and a new chapter was beginning. Very soon it would be 1965.

The crowd around him grew, people jostled and glasses clinked, and the talking and laughing became louder than ever. The excitement was rising, anticipating the climax!

Tom was jolted from his reverie as the crowd around him surged onto the street and started the countdown.

10, 9, 8, 7, 6, 5, 4, 3, 2, 1 .... Happy New Year! Everyone was shouting it out as the band burst into Auld Lang Syne. Fireworks exploded from the bridge and lit up the river. Tom watched on as happy people danced in the street. Suddenly, he was dragged from his seat and pulled into the festive crowd. Everyone was laughing, and dancing, strangers were hugging and kissing, and wishing each other a happy new year.

For a man who was used to being a loner, it was mayhem. People were tugging him in all directions and hugging him whilst laughing and singing. He looked around for a possible escape. But then, in amongst the dancers and the revellers, he saw a brunette in a black and white polka dot dress. She looked almost as uncomfortable and lost as he was. He was immediately drawn to her. When the band started playing a slow song, he walked over and shyly asked if she would like to dance.

Surprised by the stranger's invitation, she accepted. "My name is Louise," she said as he pulled her in close, protecting her from the throng of energetic dancers around them.

It felt comforting to have a woman in his arms again. They danced together for the next three dances, then found a table as far away from the band's amplifiers as they could manage. They wanted to find out about each other. But it was impossible amidst the pandemonium.

Most of what they tried to say was drowned out but at least they were able to gaze into each other's eyes. They continued to enjoy the New Year's festivities from a distance until the hotel closed.

The moon was still high and the streets were alive with New Year carousers. Not wanting to go home yet, Tom and Louise walked slowly along the river bank until the moon finally dipped and the sun brightened the horizon.

It was dawn, and they had strolled for hours, talking all the time and enjoying each other's company.

For Louise, it was a magical night. For Tom, it was sweet comfort. He was attracted to Louise and, even more, he sensed deep in his gut that they were meant to be together. He had not felt such a strong connection for a very long time. There was a stirring in his heart that had lain dormant. Maybe he was ready to think about another kind of life and leave his lonely bachelor existence behind him.

"Maybe it's time to share my life with a lovely woman like Louise," he thought as he cupped her hand gently. She came into his open arms, and he softly kissed her as the dawn broke.

On the bank of the Brisbane River, on the first day of 1965, Tom could feel himself coming alive. His body was tingling with the anticipation that he could move on from the numbness which had paralysed his emotions for so long. Louise made him feel secure, safe; she had a way about her that was warm, protective, and extremely soothing to his wounded soul. She was someone with whom he could build a good life.

Their courtship was swift. Six months later, in the winter of 1965, they married. Louise looked lovely in her flowing white dress. The reception was wonderful and her parents beamed as they bid Tom and Louise bon voyage as they departed for their honeymoon in Surfers Paradise.

The cans on the back of their car rattled along the road beneath the 'Just Married'" sign. The newly-married couple took no notice of the commotion, though, they were in a loving blissful haze of their own making.

Louise's parents were quite taken with Tom and the future he promised for their precious child. For the first six months, they lived with her parents and he was every parent's dream: sweet, quiet, polite, did not like to party, a hard worker and, most of all, he loved their daughter. They adored him.

Her parent's wedding gift to them was a parcel of land in a new area that was opening on Brisbane's northside. Almost immediately after returning from their honeymoon, Tom's spare moments were spent with a small team of friends, building the Queenslander-style 'mansion' with the bullnose awning and big sweeping verandahs at the front and sides. It was Louise's dream home that he had promised to build during their courtship.

He tried to accommodate all her wishes including the stone pillars and rail that outlined the grand staircase leading to the high-set verandah, the pitched roof and the gabled alcove and, finally, the white picket fence that framed the home perfectly.

It was finished in record time and in September '66, shortly after they officially moved into their new home, another chapter of Tom's life began as they welcomed their first child to the world.

With his shock of bright auburn hair and hazel eyes, Geoffrey Thomas Flanagan was the apple of everyone's eye. Adored by his grandparents and doted on by his mother and aunts, he was showered with more love than Tom ever believed was possible.

Having never experienced a loving, caring family, Tom began to understand how dysfunctional his own childhood had been. He made an oath to himself that his son would never feel the hurt and pain he and his siblings endured for most of their childhood.

When he looked at Geoffrey, he saw himself, what he could have been if he had grown up in a happy family. Geoffrey's face lit up every time Tom was near and his little arms reached out to him. Tom's heart was full. A loving wife, an amazing family and a son that was every man's dream.

Tom was over-the-moon happy to be a father and he cherished every milestone. He showered his son with gifts, much to his mother's disdain. Louise thought Tom was spoiling the child and that Geoffrey would grow up expecting life always to be plentiful.

She did not realise, and Tom was not aware of the reasons either, that the neglect, abuse and torture he had suffered in his childhood meant he was compensating for everything he missed out on. Tom believed he was being the best, most loving father by giving Geoffrey everything his heart desired.

He felt so proud when Geoffrey started crawling; when he took his first steps, he thought his heart might burst. Tom was content, life with Louise was pleasant, and he was satisfied with everything married life offered, but he still had a wandering spirit. A secret self that needed to be free. Being satisfied was not enough to appease his adventurous soul.

Now their house was built, he needed a new project, something he could be proud of, that gave him the opportunity to be in his own world even if only for a short time. He loved Louise, he adored Geoffrey but he craved solitude, time to think, reflect, and recharge.

Drawing on the skills learnt during his time at the shipyard, he decided that what he needed was a boat. Very soon it was beginning to take shape in his own backyard. It was apparent that that it was no rowboat he was building. At almost 30 ft long, it had a downstairs bunkhouse, intricate cabinetry in the upstairs wheelhouse and a large deck that went all the way around.

By the time Geoffrey turned two, Tom had completed and launched the boat. Louise, Geoffrey, and her parents joined him on the maiden voyage through the Moreton Bay islands. He promised more adventures as they headed for home. But taking the family by surprise, Tom soon began fishing commercially around the same islands, living for days at a time on the boat, and selling his catches at the local fish market.

He had grown tired of the house building industry and discovered instead that commercial fishing was quite lucrative. It suited him well, the solitude whilst on the water was exactly what his gypsy soul needed.

Due to the housing boom in Brisbane at that time, builders and tradespeople were in very high demand. So much work and so much money was there to be made. But because Tom chose to fish instead of build houses, he fell out of favour with Louise's parents who could not fathom his desire to leave behind his trade with its prospects of making a lot of money. Surely, the financial security of a trade and the ability to be home every night with his family were the most important things.

How could he explain to them that he felt trapped, that when he was working with others he felt like a bird in a cage? Fishing suited him perfectly. It offered him the freedom he craved although he felt guilty about spending so much time away from his son.

Periodically, he experienced flashbacks to when his own father would disappear for weeks, leaving him and his brothers alone with a mother who was irrational and often malignant. He knew Louise was nothing like his mother so in that sense Geoffrey was fine and he had the protection of loving grandparents close by.

Still, it tormented Tom to realize that he was becoming his father and there was little he could do to change it. The urge was too strong and he could not hold back the tide that kept pulling him towards the ocean.

The estrangement came on slowly. Neither Tom nor Louise realised they were drifting apart until the day came when Tom decided to take the boat further north and try fishing in the warmer tropical waters.

It came as no surprise to Louise who probably understood Tom better than Tom understood himself, and she knew that this was the way he was. She couldn't explain it, so she wasn't able to make her parents understand it. She accepted that, in order to keep Tom, she needed to let him go.

He was a solitary man. She recognised the signs of his depression, and, if he was not allowed his freedom, he would become progressively more withdrawn, frustrated and melancholy. This was not the environment she wanted for Geoffrey.

A sad depressed father was not a positive role model and to force him to stay would mean they may lose him forever. That was a chance she was not willing to take.

She was accustomed to being alone for days when he was out fishing, so she accepted his plan without question, hoping that by giving him his freedom, he would remain a part of their lives forever, in whatever form the future had in store for them.

They never fought, and hostile words never passed between them. They accepted that this separation was their future and said goodbye as Tom left Brisbane for the last time. Many people considered their relationship was unconventional but for Tom and Louise, it worked for them. They were more than content to love each other from a distance while living their separate lives.

She had their son and she knew he was the most precious thing in Tom's life, Tom had the freedom he craved. Against all her parents' predictions, he made a lucrative income trawling for prawns in the balmy North Queensland waters.

Tom's melancholy slowly lifted. When he was at sea, he was at home and no longer felt enveloped by a storm cloud that refused to lift. The savage and often unpredictable ocean became his best friend. He had set his course for the rest of his life, and that thought made him extremely happy.

The house Tom lovingly built for them and Louise lovingly decorated turned into a home which became a shrine to him.

Louise sent letters and photographs often, and created a wonderful home for Geoffrey to grow and flourish in.

Tom was never a stranger. He called on the telephone whenever he was in port and spoke to Geoffrey often, sometimes several times a week, less if he was at sea. He never forgot a birthday or Easter. At Christmas, he showered them both with extravagant gifts. Even though they lived apart, he and Louise were in many ways still very much a loving couple.

Together they raised and supported Geoffrey, offering advice to the growing lad who regaled his father with stories of his life in Brisbane. Tom, in turn, would tell Geoffrey about the new and exciting things happening on the ocean and on the boat.

Strangely enough, this arrangement worked perfectly for them all. Geoffrey thrived, growing up to be a very well-adjusted young man. His childhood was extremely happy, even without the physical guidance of a father in his life.

Chapter Twenty-Seven

The morning air was fresh, the cool breeze on her brow was a welcome relief from the heat of summer. Chiara, with Jacob by her side, was off to the post office. She had followed this same ritual on the first Monday of every month for the last year and a half.

Retrieve the cheque from the mailbox, cash it at the counter, pay the rent for the month and whatever utilities were owing before moving on to buy groceries to fill the pantry which was close to being empty at the end of each month.

Jacob ran ahead excitedly, kicking fallen leaves as he skipped along the concrete footpath.

Going to the post office was something he looked forward to every month. It meant there would be a letter from his dad and maybe a little trinket or a photograph. He loved hearing about his adventures. In his two and a half-year-old mind, his Dad had the most exciting life imaginable. He wondered what wonderful stories there would be today from the jungles of Vietnam.

Would there be monkeys and tigers again? Would he be sleeping in a funny little hut while a big elephant crashed around outside or one of those giant scary lizards?? But not his Dad! His Dad was a superhero and he fought everything and kept the camp safe because some of those animals could be nasty. That was why Dad had a gun, to keep them all safe.

"Bang, bang," Jacob called out as he fired a pretend gun, a stick he picked up from the footpath. "My dad will shoot all those lizards," he said cheerfully as he skipped along and chatted while Chiara kept a watchful eye on him to ensure he didn't run too far ahead.

Early autumn leaves were piling up on the path and crunching under her feet, as she inserted the key into the mailbox on the wall outside the post office. Jacob was excited and fidgeted while he waited for his letter and maybe a photograph.

There was nothing, the box was empty!

Chiara wrinkled her brow, confused. Martin had never missed a payment and he knew how important his letters were to Jacob. She could not understand.

"What's wrong, Mum, where's Daddy's letter?" he asked, his little hands reaching to be picked up so that he could check for himself.

"I'm afraid there is no letter, Jacob. We better ask inside. Maybe they haven't put it in the box yet."

Jacob ran into the post office and went straight to the counter, "Have you got the letter from my Daddy here?"

he asked inquisitively, jumping up to be seen above the counter. Chiara chuckled as she lifted him and sat him on the ledge. "I'm sorry about my son's rudeness, we checked the box outside but it's empty today. We thought maybe it's still here and you hadn't put it in yet?" she asked calmly.

"No, I'm sorry Mrs. Williams, there's no mail for you today."

Chiara placed a protective arm around Jacob and said, "Maybe he was so busy fighting lizards that he couldn't post it on time," all the while thinking how unusual it was. Martin had never been late before. Despite his failings, he was a good provider and never forgot his son.

Jacob was satisfied, after all his dad was a superhero. "It's OK, Mum, we'll come back and get it tomorrow," he said cheerfully. Chiara nodded, hoping her son would not be disappointed again.

Unfortunately, the next day was the same. After daily checks for the next two weeks yielded nothing, she finally accepted that the cheque was not going to arrive this month.

Chiara was worried. Had something happened to him? How will she tell Jacob? And how could she pay her debts without any funds, the bills were starting to pile up?

On the third week, she wrote a letter to the New Zealand Army. Even though she sent it by express mail, it could take weeks before she received a response. In the meantime, she must figure out how to get some money. She was afraid, and created all sorts of scenarios in her mind. What if she never heard from him again? Where will they go if they lose the cottage, how will she afford to even feed Jacob?

She cannot get a job like before, she has responsibilities, a child to look after, a home to pay for. The regular cheque from Martin was all that kept them going each month. She had no other means and there were no savings to fall back on.

And what should she tell Jacob? How long could she pretend that his dad was very busy and had not been near a post office. As young as he is, he will eventually figure out something is wrong.

She suddenly felt desperately alone, unsupported, and with a small child to care for. 'They will soon be destitute,' she worries. Everything was OK when he had a superhero dad who simply lived in another country. With the help of the letters Martin sent to Jacob, she could keep him entertained for hours with stories of his imaginary life in Vietnam. She wondered now whether she had done the right thing.

Maybe creating a fantasy father will damage his little mind irreparably when he finally discovers his Dad is not a superhero after all. Had she made the right decision not to take Jacob to New Zealand and try to be a family there? She had made so many bad choices in her life and now she was paying for it? Was this her karma for the hurt she caused in the past?

Instead of the happy future she had planned, she was being thrust into a life where she faced becoming penniless. No husband, no job, and no way to pay for the cottage, no means to support her son – and it was all her own fault. Her stomach churned, and her head was heavy. For the first time in a very long time, she was truly scared about what the future might bring.

Another month goes by and still nothing. She does not hear from anybody. It was like he had fallen off the earth and nobody was telling her anything.

Even after sending a second letter, the army still had not replied.

Jacob was asking questions, "Where is Daddy, why hasn't he written?" She didn't want to lie to her son but she also didn't want to shatter his illusions. She had no idea what to do.

Frantic at the sight of her empty pantry and the pile of unpaid bills on the table, she was becoming more and more desperate.

The second-hand shop gave her a decent payment for the heavy cot, small table, lounge, and the baby items she no longer needed, but that only paid the rent for a few weeks and a meagre amount of food. She needed a more permanent solution.

Finally, in the middle of the third month, she received word from the Army. 'Missing in Action' was the official verdict. Chiara was beside herself.

'What now, what does she tell Jacob? What does 'missing in action' even mean? Her mind was racing and nothing was making sense. Martin could still be alive somewhere. 'Was he taken prisoner? Was he being held by the enemy and unable to contact anyone?'

Standing outside the post office, Chiara scanned the page again but the words were a blur. She broke into gasping sobs, wide-eyed and staring. Swaying and about to faint, she held her arm against the wall to steady herself.

Noticing she was in distress, the postmaster brought her inside. Chiara was visibly shaking and crying. Little Jacob was frantic. He could not understand what had happened. Why was his Mum like this? The postmaster took the letter and read it for himself.

"Mrs. Williams, I am so sorry. This is horrible news."

Jacob stood quietly by her side. Not knowing what was wrong, but understanding something bad had happened. Wide-eyed, he looked at his mother as she finally began to compose herself.

"What can I do?" she asked, "I can't even pay my rent."

"Mrs. Williams, did you not see the cheque from the army? They have sent his pay to you from the last three months." She looked up, tears streaming down her red-flushed cheeks. "What?" she blurted, not able to take his words in.

"His pay. They have sent the last three months to you and will forward his next one as well until he is found." He pointed to the cheque that had fallen onto the counter. "You and your son will be OK."

"What's wrong with Daddy?" Jacob asked innocently. This remark snapped Chiara back to reality. "My God, I have to tell Jacob. "Please, do you have somewhere private we can sit?"

"Of course, my wife is inside, she'll take you to our sitting room."

Telling Jacob was the hardest thing Chiara had ever had to do. How does a mother tell her almost three-year-old son that his beloved father has gone missing?

"Why didn't he use his gun?" Jacob asked plaintively. In his mind, the lizard his dad fought was too big and he was simply hiding until it went away. Jacob believed with all his heart that his father would come out of hiding, and all would be right again in his world.

Chiara tried to explain it, but Jacob would not accept that his father may be gone for a long time and he may never hear from him again.

But Jacob was little and his dad was a superhero, and he had a gun. "It's OK, Mum, Daddy will be back soon," he said. Chiara wished she could have his childlike innocence for a few seconds because at this moment, her pain was on the verge of being unbearable. That night, and for many nights afterwards, Jacob slept with his mother. Chiara refused to let him go, terrified that. if she did, he too would vanish.

Her anxiety crushed her. She could not shake the conviction that every person who came into her life was taken from her. Thoughts of Italy, Isabella the gypsy, Tom, her baby Isabella, and now Martin flashed through her mind. She held Jacob tightly and sobbed until she finally fell into a light sleep.

The next morning, she started a plan. The three months of back pay would cover all the overdue expenses and fill the pantry again so she was happy that her finances would at least be in order – for now anyway. She had been in deep trouble, a whisker away from destitution. It made her realise that she needed a regular income. She needed a way to earn, to save, and to have an emergency fund if ever again she was left without any means of support.

She was in Brisbane, a lone woman with a husband who was missing in a war zone, a child who needed his father, a life that was mundane and frugality that was forced by circumstances.

Hastily, she penned a letter to her parents, explaining the news she had received. They were aware that he had gone to war and Chiara had never given them any reason to be concerned before. She always wrote that Jacob was happy, Martin kept in touch regularly and, although he was in Vietnam, he was safe and secure in an area that was well away from the fighting.

"It's with a heavy heart that I need to tell you I have received word that Martin is missing. I have no further information except to say he has not been found so it is possible he may be alive somewhere. Please keep him in your prayers and I will let you know any updates as soon as I hear anything."

It was a very quick letter; she licked the stamp and popped the envelope in the mailbox outside. Thoughts of returning to Cairns ran through her mind.

"Perhaps my parents will allow us to live with them until I can find my feet again." That thought was fleeting. Brisbane had become their home and this meagre cottage was all Jacob knew. All memories of his father were in this house.

Thoughts of the impact upon her from own sudden departure from everything she knew in Italy prompted her not to pursue leaving as a solution. She could not do that to Jacob. Not when he was still so little. Tearing Jacob away from the only home he had ever known would be far too traumatic.

The day after receiving her letter, Gina & Enzo decided to leave for Brisbane immediately.

Jacob opened the door after hearing a knock to see his Nonno and Nonna standing there. They swooped him up in their arms and warmly greeted Chiara who was in the tiny kitchen making a sandwich for Jacob's lunch.

Enzo is stunned to see most of the furniture gone. "I had to sell it, Papa. Martin was gone three months before I had any word, and we had no money. The furniture paid our bills."

"My dad is hiding from lizards," Jacob said nonchalantly.

Enzo's eyes became saucers and he shook his head at the mention of lizards. "Sit down Papa, we have a lot to talk about." For the rest of the afternoon, the family discussed what Chiara needs to do now. Her parents suggested a return to Cairns which she sidesteps as tactfully as possible. She explained what she would really like is not be a stay-at-home sole mother; instead, she would prefer to get a job somewhere to supplement the money from the Army. She is not sure how long Martin's army pay will last. She needs some savings to fall back on, just in case.

Her parents agreed it was a sensible plan. They were proud of how 'mature' their little tearaway had become.

"You are dealing with this difficult time very well," her father said, nodding his head vigorously.

"Yes, we are proud of you, Chiara, and, whatever you decide, we will support you," her mother added.

Chiara was overwhelmed. All her life, the only real thing she ever wanted from her parents was validation, a kind word occasionally that she was a good person despite her impetuous gypsy ways. Her parents' approval meant so much to her, especially when her life was in crisis.

The decision was made for Gina to stay and look after Jacob. Chiara knew she needed a job to be able to support them both and, while her son was young, she needed a babysitter she could trust. It worried her, she had never left Jacob alone with anybody and she was not sure she was ready to do so now. However, her mother could not stay indefinitely and, to be able to work outside the home, she had to arrange a suitable babysitter for Jacob.

The relationship with her mother had improved since Chiara became a mother, but the distance between them was often still evident. Chiara appreciated and welcomed her mother's efforts which were all to ensure she and Jacob were supported and safe. She never doubted for one second that she adored her grandson.

Slowly but surely, Chiara came to see her mother in a very different light. Being a mother herself, she began to understand how complicated that relationship can be, especially when there are things you can never discuss with your child. Things like the real reason their home was burnt to the ground, or why they were hiding in a cellar beneath a hotel for a week, or who the official looking strangers were that visited them every night and why they left Italy so suddenly and had someone in Australia waiting for their arrival.

Chiara looked back through her adult eyes, realizing what a desperate, dangerous time for her parents. It obviously involved major criminals. Putting herself in the position her parents must have been in, it struck her like a bolt of lightning that it was done to protect her. There had been no choice but to flee. Their reasons were irrelevant. Her parents took huge decisions to ensure that she was safe and could live a life free from the dangers they left behind in Italy.

Now she was grown up and able to process the events, Chiara understood there was so much her parents had kept from her because they were, and still are, protecting her. Their protection was born from a deep love and a desire to keep her safe, regardless of the costs to themselves. Her baby girl, Isabella, wasn't taken because her parents were ashamed. They did what was best for her and their grandchild. Chiara could never give Isabella the opportunities that financially stable and happily married parents could.

At seventeen, she was still a child. She realised that now and finally understood that everything in life changes when you become a parent. Shielding those you love from outside hurt is what parents do. It's what her parents did for her and it is what she is doing for Jacob by turning his father into a superhero who fought lizards in the jungles of Vietnam.

Chapter Twenty-Eight

*B*ella 1966: The sun was peeping over the horizon. Bella giggled as she sat up in her bed. She knew she was awake before Mama and Papa because the streaks of pink and lavender tinting the morning sky. Her room was filled with the rosy hue that only the dawn can bring.

The bright sun sent shards of golden light which refracted like precious jewels through the glass butterflies hanging from the window and caught the particles of dust shimmering like fairy sprinkles as they glided on the breeze. Each morning, the colour of the sunrise changed and consequently, so did the glass butterflies.

It was quiet and still dark in the house. The magical kaleidoscope of the dawn was just for her and it made her heart sing. The gentle breeze tickled the curtains, as she breathed in the warm country air wafting through her bedroom window.

"Good morning, Mr. Sunshine," she said in her best sing-song voice. "Thank you for another beautiful morning." A kookaburra laughed outside, heralding the new day and she looked across at George and Faye tucked snugly into their cradle.

"Good morning George, good morning Faye, guess what? Today is special. I'm going to school today." She had been looking forward to this day for weeks. Finally, she will be in grade one with all her friends from kindergarten. She could not wait.

She picked up her story book from the little table beside the doll house. Sitting cross-legged on the floor, Bell began to recite what she remembered from the story Mama read to her last night.

"George and Faye, you must listen carefully. This story is very important because it's all about a little girl who was given to somebody else who really wanted her to live with them. Her name is Pollyanna and she went to live with her new family in the country. Mama said she was like me, that her new mama and papa loved her more than anything in the whole wide world and she would live with them forever and ever."

A big black Labrador wandered in and flopped down beside her on the floor. "Good morning, Cora, you need to be quiet because I'm telling George and Faye all about this girl in my storybook," she said, as her faithful doe-eyed friend laid her curly head on her lap.

"Do you remember when we got Cora?" Bella said to her dolls. "Cora's Mum had lots of puppies and when Cora was big enough, we took her home to live with us" she said innocently. "That is what happens, George and Faye, when a baby is big enough, they go to a family that really wants them, just like me. Mama and Papa really wanted me, so they chose me from lots of other babies and took me to their home to live with them forever," she said wistfully looking at the fading dawn and how the room was filling with bright sunlight.

She heard soft footsteps moving around in the kitchen. "Mama's awake, we need to go and say good morning." She scooped the dolls up from their cradle, and wandered out with Cora close behind as usual.

Ava's eyes lit up and her face broke into a warm smile at the sight of her five-year-old daughter clutching her dolls in both arms and her dog beside her.

'She gets more beautiful every day,' she thought as she looked at Bella's tumbling copper curls and large brown eyes. 'How did we get so lucky?' she wondered as she knelt to give her beloved daughter a hug. "Good morning, my darling, are you excited? Today will be your first day at school, you are growing up so quickly," she said as she pushed Bella's hair back and softly kissed her forehead.

"Papa is going out to get the eggs. If you're quick, you can go with him." Bella's eyes lit up; she loved the chicken pen. There was one rooster that everybody hated because he would chase anyone who came through the gate, but he would always sit for Bella so she could pick him up while Papa checked for eggs.

Leaving the dolls with her mother, she skipped across the lawn, Cora running beside her and sitting as they reached the gate. "Good morning, Papa," she said brightly as she entered the gate.

"Oh, my Bella Butterfly, just who I need, the rooster is being extra cranky today." Right on cue, the rooster squatted in front of her and she scooped him up in her arms whilst Nico collected the eggs.

Together they walked back to the house, Bella chatting non-stop about the kangaroos she spotted in the distance. She called Cora back as she barked loudly and ran off to chase them.

Quickly finishing her breakfast, Bella ran to the car to wait for her parents, excited that she would soon be at the school. A short trip later, she said goodbye to her father as he drove off to work after dropping them at the school gates.

Hand in hand, she walked in confidently with her mother, more than ready to begin the first day of her school life. Bella had never gone anywhere previously without her mother and her dog by her side. But she was prepared. School would be an adventure and she couldn't wait any longer.

As they went through the gates, her confidence suddenly crumbled. Her tummy felt funny, everything was much bigger than she thought it would be. There were so many other children, many of them much older than her, and she snuggled in against her mother.

"It's going to be fine, amore, I'll walk you in to your classroom today," Ava said. "Be brave, my little butterfly." Upon hearing these words, Bella felt a surge of courage. She inhaled deeply, clutched her brown school case in one hand and, with her head held high, marched proudly to the grade one classroom. Placing her case on the rack, she hugged her mother goodbye.

The bell rang, her mother left, and she was alone. A little lost coppertop in a small sea of other equally-bewildered first graders.

Miss Owen was her teacher, and Bella thought she was very pretty. Just like a princess and she was nice to everyone.

That first week was a whirlwind, she was sitting at a desk, watching Miss Owen write something on the blackboard, then wipe it off with her special chalk duster. Bella picked up her slate and practised writing, chatted to Billy in the seat beside her, counted with coloured rods, and chanted the two times table with the rest of the class.

At 10 a.m., they stopped for little lunch and she drank the little bottle of milk. At big lunch, her once-a-week treat was a meat pie from the tuck-shop, but most days it was Vegemite sandwiches and a piece of fruit from the brown paper bag her mother packed each morning. If there was time after eating, she would play games with her new friends in the playground. After the final bell at 3 p.m., she would sit under the big jacaranda tree waiting for her mother to arrive and they would walk home together.

School was only scary that first morning. She played skip rope and hopscotch with her new friends Karen and Joanne, and spun around on the merry-go-round, giggling when she was so dizzy that she couldn't walk straight after getting off it.

School was fun and she made lots of friends in those first few weeks. In the afternoons, some bigger children were often close by, but they usually sat in a group away from where Bella and her friends played.

One afternoon one of boys ventured over. His name was Peter and he was horrid to everybody. "You were adopted," he said.

Bella looked confused; she did not understand. Of course she was adopted, everybody is adopted, that is how we end up with our families. In Bella's mind, every child was adopted, just like a puppy or a kitten. When they get bigger, a mum and dad choose which one they want and they take them home with them. That was the reality she had created in her mind, so the words from this boy made no sense to her.

"You were adopted because you were a migrant and your mother didn't want to keep you," he said cruelly.

"But my mother does want me; she's picking me up soon," Bella was close to tears. She felt confused and upset. 'What was this boy saying? '

"Not that mother, silly, your real mother."

Bella was baffled. What was he saying? Mama is my real mother. The taunts continued. Little Bella became more confused, her chin trembled and she began to cry.

That afternoon, she asked her mother what the boy meant. "He said my real mother didn't want me because I was a migrant. Mama, you are my real mother, I don't understand," she said tearfully.

"Oh Bella" she exclaimed as she scooped her daughter up into her arms, hugging her tightly. "Sometimes people are not nice because they don't understand. They say cruel

and horrible things because they envy what you have."
Ava was distraught seeing her daughter so distressed.

"What does envy mean?"

"It's when you have something that somebody else
wishes they had"

"Why does he envy me?" she asked, adding "What's
a migrant, mama?" Bella became more and more upset
as she tried to work everything out in her head.

"A migrant is a person that was born in another
country. He envies you because you are so special and
precious to Papa and I."

"Doesn't his mama and papa think he is special and
precious too"

Ava gave her a smile, "I am sure they do."

Until now, Bella's life had been a happy existence of
sunshine, flowers, and butterflies. She didn't like how
this boy had made her feel. It had frightened her.

Ava hated that she could not hug this pain away
for Bella. The time had come, she realised, for her and
Nico to have a serious conversation with their young
daughter.

That night Bella learnt that the boy was a little bit
right when he said she was different to all the other children but she also learnt that this made her even more
special because she had two mothers and two fathers
and everybody loved her dearly.

She learnt that she grew in the tummy of her first
mother until she was big enough to be born and then
she was cared for by a nurse in a special hospital with
lots of other babies.

Even though her first mother loved her dearly, she was not able to care for Bella properly as she had no money. She couldn't buy the things Bella would need and, because she loved Bella so much, she gave her to her new mama and papa so that she would have the best life she could possibly have. She chose us because she knew we wanted you so badly and would love you forever."

She also learnt that the boy was very wrong when he said her mother gave her away because she was a migrant. "Your first mother is Italian, like we are," said Ava. "She said to the nurse, that she wanted you to grow up with us, so that you would always know how special it is to be Italian. She chose Isabella as your name, and we thought the name suited you perfectly."

Nico added, "You must never forget it was because she loved you so much, that she gave you to us. For that special gift, we will always be grateful and she will always have a special place in our hearts and prayers." All night Bella asked questions, and all night her parents answered them as honestly as they could, making sure she understood how blessed she was because not every child is as lucky as Bella. Not every child is a gift and she was the best gift of all.

The next morning Bella went to school with a new confidence.

She had something that no other child had, and it made her exceptional.

Her first mother loved her so much, and wanted Bella to have the things she couldn't give her so she gave her to a Mama and Papa who would look after her and love her forever. She was a gift to them and had arrived in their home two days after her Mama's birthday. She was 12 days old.

Bella lifted her head proudly. She was adopted, and that made her feel very happy, so when the boys tried to taunt her again, she stood tall, looked straight at them, and said, "Yes, I am adopted and I have two mothers and two fathers; so, I have twice as many people who love me and I was a gift. My Mama and Papa chose me to be their forever child." The little five-year-old proved at that moment that her spirit was as strong and feisty as the gypsies back in Italy.

She had a wisdom far beyond her tender years and, although she didn't realise it yet, that resilience and determined nature would take her to many places in her life.

Bella Butterfly was destined for a bright and happy future.

Chapter Twenty-Nine

Chiara woke early, refreshed from her most restful sleep in many months and feeling positive about the day that lay ahead. Finally, she could move forward from the uncertainty of her day-to-day existence. She looked fondly at her young son, still sleeping soundly in the bed beside her. "Jacob is growing so fast," she thought.

As each day passed, he was becoming more and more like his father. His black eyes, thick black hair, olive skin and the very same flat nose with wide nostrils that flared every time he took a breath.

Watching him, she had flashbacks to their days in West End, Martin did the very same thing and she found it so intoxicating, and now Jacob had the exact same habit, his nostrils flared like his father's even though he never really knew him or spent time with him. Chiara was amazed that Jacob was a replica of him, his character, his personality, his looks and even his mannerisms.

It was as if Martin was still with her. She missed him, even though the fights were bad, and the distance was horrible, but the spark they had was undeniable. She wondered if she would ever experience that again. Chiara marvelled at how fast time had moved. She could not believe that Jacob was already a three-year-old. Four years had passed since she and Martin first met.

It was October 1967 and, as happened every October, she remembered the first time she brought a child into the world. 'Isabella would be turning seven,' she mused. "She would have started school already. I wonder if her parents had a party for her birthday." In her mind's eye, she could see a little girl who looked like Tom, with freckles and tumbling orange curls, happily blowing out candles on a tall cake covered in pink and white frosting while her family sang a happy birthday song. This vision made her happy, she hoped Isabella had the life she deserved.

Her son stirred beside her, wiping the sleep from his eyes, and smiling at his mother as she embraced him lovingly. She adored her son but still longed for the secret daughter she was not allowed to keep.

Gina appeared in the doorway, grinning, with a scalding pot of espresso in her hand, the intoxicating aroma of fresh coffee was one she had almost forgotten. It had been a long time. Yesterday, her mother excitedly showed off the purchase she made from the second-hand store, a genuine Italian stove top percolator.

Sitting at the table, watching her mother vigorously shake hot milk in a jar until it was frothy, ladling it over the steaming coffee in her cup and inhaling the aroma of fresh bread toasted over the hot coals of the wood stove. Slathered with butter and jam, it brought back a long-forgotten memory of a little girl about Jacob's age sitting at a table somewhere in Italy, sharing breakfast with her Nonna and Mama.

With Jacob clumsily spreading jam on his thick slab of home-baked bread, a glass of fresh milk in front of him and the adults sharing a pot of fresh coffee, it was the breakfast from her childhood. She had not realised how much she missed it.

They chatted about the plans for the day. Chiara thought she would start by asking at the post office and checking the newspaper for vacancies. Gina mentioned that her plan was to take Jacob to the back yard and pick mulberries from the huge tree and maybe make some jam or a sweet pie for after dinner tonight.

Chiara licked her lips. Oh, to be a child again, picking berries sounded like so much fun, but she had work to do. She kissed her son good-bye, told him to enjoy his day with Nonna and left for the morning.

She quickly found out about several factories that were always looking for workers. The first one, a fruit cannery, was a short tram ride from home. Workers had to be on site at 6.30 a.m. to register. If the quota was full, they would not work that day.

The other factory produced breakfast cereal and, although it was also casual, it was not on the same first-in basis as the cannery. However, it was located on the other side of the city, an hour's tram ride away. Since the cannery was closest, she decided to try there in the morning. That afternoon, she started her quest for a babysitter.

Speaking again with the postmaster, she penned a small sign to place on the bulletin board, checked the other advertisements for any other work that may be suitable, but there was only hotel work. She missed the hotel, but with a child, it was out of the question and there was nothing else that was suitable for a young single mother.

The afternoon ended with a visit to her favourite Italian greengrocer, having a quick chat with the owner, purchasing the ingredients for a risotto that her mother had requested and discussing the method for pillowy gnocchi, with a delicious green pesto or a fresh tomato and garlic sauce.

She remembered these recipes from her childhood and, as she walked home, laden with paper bags filled with fresh ingredients, she made a mental note to ask her mother to write down all her recipes before she returned to Cairns.

It was late afternoon when she arrived home, the house smelt wonderful as the tantalizing aroma of sweet pie met her at the door. Covered in mulberry juice, Jacob's grin was as wide as his purple-stained face as he stood on the kitchen chair beside his Nonna, stirring the pot of jam simmering on the stove. He seemed so happy, and Chiara noted he didn't ask about his father as soon as she walked in, nor did he mention lizards or elephants, or whatever else his father might be hiding from.

That night, they feasted on a deliciously creamy risotto, sweet mulberry pie and homemade gelato and, with full tummies, they retired early. At 5 a.m. Chiara was on her way to the cannery. As luck would have it, she made the quota, settled into the routine of assembly line work and eight hours later she was picking up her pay. For the next week, she repeated the cycle, working at the cannery, stopping at the greengrocer for supplies and checking on her advertisement at the post office.

Finally, at the start of the second week, she had a response with a name and address waiting at the post office. The postmaster informed Chiara that the applicant was a well-known, respected older woman with grown children. She had started a child-minding service in her home.

Chiara was apprehensive but she knew if she wanted to continue to work, she needed to find arrangements for Jacob as his Nonna would be leaving soon.

The woman's home was close, an old weatherboard cottage like her own but obviously well-loved and meticulously maintained, with a well-kept yard at the front. A children's play area was down the side with swings with a sandpit underneath a large shady tree. Her name was Joyce Carruthers, or 'Mama J' as she was known by the children. She was a large-bodied, motherly figure with a friendly face and a happy disposition. Chiara felt instantly comfortable with her and decided she would bring her mother and Jacob to meet her on the following afternoon.

Gina was equally taken by the 'quaint' cottage that oozed family and home, but she was a little concerned about the way Mama J. was walking. They discussed whether her portly frame was becoming too much for her aging joints to bear. Would it be an issue when she was caring for a boy as spirited as Jacob? Nevertheless, Mama

J. and Jacob connected almost immediately, and Jacob quickly settled in the sandpit with the other children.

The adults enjoyed a cup of tea and biscuits on the verandah and chatted about the arrangements. After settling on a price, it was agreed that Jacob would start the very next day with his grandmother overseeing for the first few days.

That week Chiara bonded with her mother in a way she never had before. She finally felt safe, Jacob was being protected by her mother and he was never going anywhere his mother didn't agree to. Something calming was happening deep in her heart which had been pulled from a deep freeze and was beginning to warm up once again.

The pain of Martin was fading, and she was ready to forgive her mother for forcing her to give up Isabella. But she was still not ready to talk about that dark period in her life.

At daybreak, they would walk together to Mama J's house, and watch Jacob skip up the path to join the other children for breakfast. Gina would return home until the afternoon when they would meet again at Mama J's for the pickup.

Life was still mundane, but Chiara was beginning to like it that way. It had a structure and a familiarity that was comforting.

Chapter Thirty

Chiara strolled contentedly along the footpath enjoying the warmth of the sun on her back. Late March always felt like a special time of the year. Autumn leaves were beginning to flash bronze and red in the golden light of late afternoon.

She heard the children's laughter as she approached Mama J's house and Jacob's shrill voice demanding to be pushed higher on the swing.

'Hmm, I wonder who that man is, I haven't seen him before,' she mused as she walked over to greet Mama J.

"Chiara, this is my son, Robert, and these are my grandchildren." She fondly tapped each one on the head as she introduced them.

"Michelle is 10, Susan is almost 9, Leanne turned 7 yesterday and this little ratbag is Colin. He's 5."

Colin scowled, "Granny, I'm not a ratbag." They both laughed as he climbed onto her lap for a quick snuggle.

It was clear Joyce adored her grandchildren and her son relished the attention she gave them.

There was something though. She couldn't quite figure out what it was but there was a sadness in his eyes.

"Robert will be living here for a while until he can find a house," Mama J said.

"Did you move from somewhere else?" Chiara quizzed.

"Yes, we had a farm near Roma in central Queensland."

"Chiara noticed he was wearing a wedding ring and wondered where his wife might be. "Is your wife out shopping?" she asked, trying to appear nonchalant.

"My wife passed away," he replied in a matter-of-fact way. "I'm showing the kids where I grew up." Again, that sadness. It was like a veil

"I'm so sorry," said Chiara. "I shouldn't pry".

"It's OK," he said. "Jean died two years ago so we are used to people asking questions. It seems a sole father of four is quite a novelty," he stated with more than a hint of sarcasm.

The air became thick, the silence deafening. Chiara shuffled from side to side, wanting to flee but not wishing to appear rude. Thankfully, Jacob interrupted them as he ran up the stairs to greet his mother.

Whispering a silent 'thank you' and smiling sweetly at her son, she announced, "I had better get this little man home, I'll see you in the morning Mama J."

"Yes, bright and early. The kids are making pancakes in the morning."

As they walked up the path, she could sense Robert's eyes following her.

She liked the attention and felt intrigued by him as well. Not like it was with Tom, not even like Martin. This felt different. This felt soothing. This felt like liniment for an aching soul.

One quick stop to check the mailbox on the way home. There was a letter and it was from the New Zealand army.

She looked at her son, her heart racing as she tore the envelope open.

The letter advised that Martin's remains had been found. Several bodies were discovered in a mass grave close to an enemy camp. They believed he was taken prisoner and died from an undetermined cause.

His body had been identified, and arrangements were now being made for his belongings to be sent back to her in Australia.

Strangely, she was unmoved. She expected that, when she finally received some news, she would be sad. Now she had the closure she craved, why was she not affected emotionally? ?

Could it be that she already did most of her grieving after she received the first letter?

Was she so emotionally drained that she could no longer process bad news?

It was strange how she couldn't cry for the man who, not so long ago, she would have given her life for. He was her son's father, and now she must turn him into a new super persona who died a hero. That image would stay alive in her son's mind forever.

The letter explained that she would now receive a war widow's pension. It was less than Martin's salary but, thankfully with the small savings she had tucked away and her job, she will be able to maintain a comfortable existence for herself and Jacob.

After she received the news of Martin's death, life moved on quickly. Chiara broke the news of his father's death to Jacob and he took it surprisingly well. Fortunately, he was still young enough not to grasp the full meaning. He decided that maybe the lizard he fought was just too big this time. His Dad was still a superhero.

Martin's belongings arrived at the beginning of winter; his identity tags, a duffel bag with a few items of clothing, a watch, a beaten leather wallet which contained a photo of Chiara and himself taken in happier times and another of Jacob. A poem from a book she didn't recognise. All the letters she sent and a letter he had written with 100 pounds folded inside it. It detailed how he was moving to another camp. He said, "It's pretty bad over here at the moment, but as soon as I can, I will send this money to you."

A week later, Gina and Enzo arrived to help their daughter get Martin's affairs in order.

Everything moved faster than expected and the next three months were a blur.

Because he was a New Zealand citizen, there would be no official ceremony in Australia. However, an officer of the Australian Army attended the memorial service in his honor and presented the New Zealand Memorial Cross to Martin posthumously.

Chiara never felt prouder than when her now four-year-old son stood tall and marched to the front to accept the medal on behalf of his father. She honestly thought her heart might burst when he stood back and saluted. It was a moment that would be etched into her memory forever.

Mama J was there, with the Post Office people and the grocers. Even Ross and Veronica, who were still in West End, attended and the hotel publican where she worked and first met Martin, quietly took a back seat in the small chapel. She was overwhelmed by the number of people who came to show their respects.

Many were from his work, some from the hotel he frequented and they all spoke fondly of him. They mentioned how he spoke well of Chiara and Jacob which honestly surprised her. She had no idea. She always thought that, because of the fights, he hated her.

After the service, Gina, Enzo, Chiara and Jacob joined Robert at Mama J's house for a small wake. Maybe it was the commonality of losing someone they loved, maybe it was shared grief, but something brought Chiara and Robert together that afternoon.

Enzo was wary. It was now a third relationship and his daughter was not yet twenty-five. Gina was a little less skeptical. She thought Robert was a good man who clearly loved his children. He would be good for Jacob as he grew older and started looking for a male role model.

The relationship blossomed. It was comfortable. Not the desperate comfort she shared with Tom, nor the lustful comfort she shared with Martin. This was deeper. It felt real and it felt right.

Robert taught her how to drive his car and she turned out to be a natural. Within weeks, she had a licence. With the help of Martin's army payout, she was able to buy herself a small car. It wasn't much, in fact it was pretty small and beaten up and reminded her of the cane toads in Cairns, but it was hers and she loved it.

The ability to drive anywhere, to explore new parts of Brisbane and to take Jacob on excursions to waterfalls and have picnics in the forest was immeasurable.

One day, she thought, she might even drive him to Cairns to show him where she spent much of her childhood.

In February, Robert settled on a large farmhouse with acreage, just outside of Ipswich.

In March 1969, they married.

Finally, she packed up her old life, bit by bit. Robert was so patient as she filled the back of his station wagon with her bright orange furniture and the many boxes of knick-knacks she had accumulated.

A large timeworn brown suitcase contained her scarves and all the memories she had collected and displayed around the home. Everything else was packed into the cane toad with Jacob. Together, Chiara, Robert and Jacob drove off to start the next chapter of their lives.

Twelve months later, sitting in the garden in the cool of the evening, almost three months into the new decade, Chiara reflected on everything that happened since she and her parents arrived in Australia in 1956.

After fourteen years, she was an Australian but her heart was still Italian. After all, it was her feisty Italian spirit that kept her going through the most difficult times of her life. In spite of it all, she had not been broken.

Domesticity was proving to be a sweet solace from the whirlwind of her life since she left Cairns. To her astonishment, she thrived. Seeing all the children playing happily. Their family seamlessly blended as one.

For fleeting moments, her thoughts lingered on Tom and she wondered what had happened to him. Where was he, her soulmate? Was he happy? What of his large family? How did they all grow up? Irene would be a teen in high school. She closed her eyes and drifted further back.

Her mind floated to the gypsy camp and Isabella. How joyously they danced to the melodic accordion. Childhood memories of a time when life was free and natural.

Then she was on a ship, a train, and living in little green house they called home. Muffled sounds of a baby she would never meet, and the first visit from her parents when she told them of her marriage. How they doted on little Jacob. They never knew Martin had left her, only that he was called to war and never returned.

She thought fondly of the time when her parents said they were proud of her. Her own pride in seeing her four-year-old son salute an officer in honor of his father.

Maturity gave her acceptance and wisdom; serenity claimed her mind. Yet simmering below the surface was her restless soul that ached for more adventure.

The baby girl born when she was seventeen would always be her private cross to bear. Only her parents knew about her other child, her daughter Isabella. Was that still her name or had it been changed? Where was she now? Was she being well cared for? So many questions would remain unanswered.

In her mind's eye, her daughter would always be 'her Isabella.' She imagined a little girl almost ten years old with copper-coloured hair playing hopscotch with her friends, giggling and jumping on one leg. Like her, Isabella would be blessed and cursed with an adventurous, inquisitive spirit.

A red and black butterfly landed on her hand and gently fanned its wings. It was so delicate and beautiful. At that moment, in her heart she knew her Isabella was happy.

Sadness had tinged her life, but that sadness brought her to Robert. She finally understood. She no longer yearned for freedom or for the days of her youth. The butterfly in front of her was the beacon lighting the path. It was her Bella Butterfly ... the same butterfly that always appeared at the most tumultuous times in her life. It showed her that she was on the right path to contentment and happiness in her life.

Shaking herself out of her reverie, Chiara looked down at the newborn daughter she cradled in her arms. Kissing her baby's soft cheek, she whispered, "Welcome to our world, Gina Maria. One day, I will tell you the story of my life, for now it's enough for you to know you are cherished and loved, forever in the bosom of your family." Everything was as it was meant to be.

About the Author

This story began before I was born. Whilst based on facts, the inspiration came from my love of writing fiction. Now in my sixties, it was time for me to break away from pure fiction. Although the names and certain circumstances have been altered, it was time to tell my parents' story through their eyes and how I came to be.

www.ingramcontent.com/pod-product-compliance
Lightning Source LLC
Chambersburg PA
CBHW070338260626
47160CB00003B/1078